I Met Him in the Ladies' Room

A Novella
By Michelle Stimpson

Published by MLStimpson Enterprises
MichelleStimpson.com
Michelle@MichelleStimpson.com

For my family in the faith

Acknowledgments

I give glory to God for His love. Thank You for revealing Yourself to me, in Christ, at a higher level every single day. I understand now why the old saints sang, "Every day with Jesus is sweeter than the day before."

Thanks to my writing group for your encouragement. I've been putting off this delightful story for a little over four years now. Thanks, April, for your fine encouragement and editing. Thanks especially to fellow author Kellie Gilbert, who harassed me until I could ignore her no longer. Tag, you're it!

I'm thankful to my daughter, son and husband, who allowed me to punch it out, even over the Christmas holidays.

Thanks to all of my readers who continue to encourage me with your e-mail messages and sweet Facebook posts. You are wonderful!

In His Service,
Michelle Stimpson
January, 2013

Chapter 1

Christmas was the only "religious" thing we did as a family, if you could call what we did religious. Somehow, a six-pack of beer and a stolen Atari system under the tree seemed to detract from the sacred nature of the celebration.

How did I know it was sacred? They cancelled school for it. We also got out for Thanksgiving and Good Friday, but those two never quite caught on in my family.

So, years later, when my roommate Stephanie printed off a vacancy announcement from a local church which stated one of the requirements for employment was *Applicants must have accepted Christ as personal Savior and be committed to continuous spiritual growth* I yelled at her, "Did you read *this* part?"

"What part?" Stephanie asked, plopping herself down on my bed. Snatching the paper back from me, she pushed her jet-black hair behind both ears and took a second look at the post.

"This part right here," I punched the paper to point out criteria number six, "about being a Christian."

She grabbed my hand and inspected my fingers instead of the job description. "You need a manicure."

In protest, I folded my hands beneath my armpits. "Get serious. I've got less than a year to get a job and get myself established."

"What kind of job do you expect to get with nails like these?" She smirked. "Gardener, maybe? Ditch-digger?"

I returned her smirk with what I thought was one of my own, but I'm sure it looked more like a smile. Stephanie, ever-cheerful, had jokes for everything. She also had good looks and a rich, functional family—attributes that totally escaped me. No wonder people like her were in love and engaged. The only wonder was how we ended up best friends and how she'd all but supported me since we graduated from junior college. Now that she was getting married to Ricardo, I had to be a grown-up. We'd both have to be grown-ups, we gathered. For her: no more running to Daddy. For me: no more running to Stephanie. Hence, my dire need for steady employment.

Stephanie re-read the requirements and then announced, "Kerri, you can *so* be a Christian. It's not that big a deal from what I can tell. You believe in God, right?"

"Yeah, me and every other heathen," I joked.

Stephanie smacked the papers on the bed, straightened her back, and walked me through her rationale. "Didn't you, like, go to church when you were little?"

"Nnnnnope," the word slid out of me.

"Okay," she said with a clap of her hands, "Did you ever say bedtime prayers?"

"Aaanck."

"Get baptized?"

"Strike three, Stephanie, I'm out. You can't just *be* a Christian. You gotta, like, take all these classes and stuff. You remember Danny?" I referenced an ex-boyfriend of mine who wasn't necessarily spiritual but was definitely a repository of useless information.

"He said you have to get this kit and memorize volumes of prose and drink wine before you can become a confirmed Christian."

Stephanie's perfectly shaped eyebrows shot up an inch. "You've had wine! And remember that Catholic wedding we went to? We drank wine there."

"I am not a Christian, and I am not going to fake like one just so I can get a job. I might as well be...a politician or something," I said.

Fourteen days and six job rejection notifications later, I found myself running for the office of "Writer/Editor" at one of the largest churches in the Dallas area. Sure, my conscious bothered me. Actually, it did more than bother me, it harassed me. So much that I'd added "Become a Christian" to the top of my list of "Things to Do Today" every day for the last week. I never quite got around to it though, since I couldn't get in touch with Danny for the books or the wine to get the job done.

When the lady from the church called to confirm the interview, all I could do was hope like crazy I wouldn't have to take some kind of Christian-test as part of the screening process.

As I waited for my potential boss to call me beyond the reception area, I browsed the church's magazine rack. Each issue boasted the picture of a distinguished, deeply brown-skinned man with the salt-and-pepper hair one only gets with years of wisdom. His wife, clad in an elegant dress suit, was equally impressive. Stephanie would say she was quietly wealthy.

They were, upon further inspection, pastor and wife of Wesley Street Bible Fellowship; Pastor and Mrs. Scott. I had done some research about the church online, but the picture on the webpage didn't do them justice.

I flipped through one of the magazines, still awaiting my interview, and came across a brief clip entitled, "How to Accept Christ as your Personal Savior." My heart screeched to a halt. Yes! I'd found it! I breezed to the bottom of the article to find the kit-ordering information. There was no time to lose. If I could order the kit *before* the interview, I would only have to tell a partial lie about this whole "being a Christian" thing. As long as my Christian kit was on the way, I was half-way home.

I jumped from the cushy chair and approached the office secretary. She slung her floppy bangs away from her eyes and asked, "Yes?"

"Sorry to bother you, but where's the ladies' room?"

She pointed to the left. "Around this corner – two doors down."

"Thanks."

With the magazine still in hand, I entered the bathroom and rushed into the first stall, determined to break this secret code and find out how I could get my hands on the information. There had to be an 800-number or something! I re-read the clip in its entirety, slowly this time. Was it really that simple? Say this prayer and then – POOF! –bad stuff be gone, you're a Christian?

It cannot be this simple.

Whatever. If this is what they wanted, this is what they would get. I searched the bathroom with my ears, and when I determined there was no one else around, I whispered the printed prayer:

Jesus, I come to you as a sinner, confessing my sins, and asking for your forgiveness. I believe you died on the cross for my sins, you rose again, and you are now seated at the right hand of God. I invite you to come into my heart and be my personal savior. Amen.

Then I waited. I don't really know why or what for, I just waited. After a few minutes, I realized I was probably waiting to be struck by lightning for doing such a bad deed. I didn't know much about God, but I figured it was pretty safe to say that He didn't like phonies. Who was I kidding? I couldn't take this job. Not like *this*. Not if I didn't really mean what I'd said.

I guess that was the part that got me – how could I believe in something I didn't really understand? Who exactly was this Jesus dude? If he died and then got back up again, did that make him an angel like Grandpa Skeeter? When Grandpa Skeeter died, everyone said he turned into a guardian angel. In life, he always carried a .45, which, I supposed, made him a prime candidate to be guardian of something or another.

Who said I was a sinner, anyway? Okay, I had bad credit, but that was all thanks to a former boyfriend who convinced me to add him to my cell phone plan and co-sign for a Nissan. Never mind that I couldn't even drive it because it had manual transmission. No, I wouldn't classify my credit score as sin. I'd just been plain old stupid.

I heard the bathroom door swing open and listened as a pair of pumps stomped two steps inside. "Miss Dalee?"

"Yes," I answered.

"Are you okay?"

My mind scrambled back to reality. "Yes, I'm okay. I'm just...finishing up." I reached behind myself and flushed the toilet for effect. Not quite sure what effect I was going for.

"Mrs. Trenton will see you now."

"I'll be right out."

Time to lie? Or not? I stepped out of the stall and into a forced meeting with myself because the wall-length mirror was now directly across from me. My deep brown hair swung low at my cheekbones, accenting a sharp V-chin and nearly overpowering my face.

Stephanie always said my hair was too big for me, as were my feet. Everything in between the two hadn't changed much since the seventh grade. Makeup helped to bring out my hazel eyes a little, but Maybelline and Max Factor can only do so much. My only "interview" suit swallowed me and probably would have overcome me if I hadn't pinned the skirt at the waist.

The woman staring back at me was...well, I didn't really think of myself as a woman. A woman has confidence. Wisdom. Girth. This girl in the mirror felt as insecure and silly and painstakingly skinny as I had ever been, only now I could safely add dishonest to my list descriptors.

"No," I said out loud to myself. This was as good a time as any for a pep talk. I stepped up to the glass and gave myself a what-would-Stephanie-say? lecture.

"You prayed the prayer, you *wanted* to mean it...you just don't know what it means. They can't count off for that. You'll find out what it means later. Now, build a bridge and get over it 'cause you need this job, girlie."

I didn't know what to say next, so I quoted my favorite line from *The Lion King.* "It is time."

Chapter 2

Mrs. Trenton looked exactly the way I figured a "Mrs. Trenton" would look. She had that "teacher" feel to her – like she might spring a pop quiz at any moment. She was fair skinned, with light brown hair pulled into a loose ponytail, a somewhat hefty build, and killer gray eyes which she hid behind a pair of oversized glasses. She looked like one of those people in an Extreme Makeover "before" shot where I think to myself: she's not *that* bad – they could have found somebody worse off to give a makeover.

But I had to stop thinking weird thoughts. I was a Christian now, whatever that meant. I responded to her greeting with, "Hello, Mrs. Trenton. It's nice to meet you as well."

"Oh, call me Irene." She waved off the formals and I noticed her bright smile. Okay, now she was one of those fun teachers – the type everyone remembers not because they were the hardest or the trendiest, but because they actually cared about you. Even if I failed her pop quiz, she would tutor me. I liked her already. Too bad I had to lie to her.

I followed her to her office, small-talk all the way, and she finally sat across from me at her desk. Her office was decorated with pictures of her family; a husband and *four* kids. *Who has four kids these days?*

The room had a distinctly peachy smell and I couldn't figure out where it was coming from which kind of bugged me. Nonetheless, it was time for the interview.

"Kerri Du-*lee*?" Irene struggled to pronounce my name.

"Actually, it rhymes with Bailey."

"Oh," she said and then pronounced it correctly. "My apologies."

"No problem. It happens all the time."

She started the interview with, "I've looked over the work you submitted and I have to say, I'm very impressed."

"Thank you. I've always loved writing."

Irene nodded as she continued to review the material I had included with my online resume. I'd attached several typed memos and a flyer I created for a non-profit organization. At that point, my publishing credits consisted of three articles for the local paper and two poems published by a company I later learned was a scam. Hopefully, only me and the other totally green writers who paid the fee to enter and then bought the book we're published in know this small fact.

Irene slapped my manila folder closed and laced her fingers. "Well, I'm sure your writing skills are up to par. I'd like to hear more about *Kerri*."

I gave my usual spiel: I'm originally from Colorado. My family moved to Oklahoma in the late 90's. I went to junior college in Texas, then took a job as an administrative assistant at a water purification company that announced its bankruptcy the day I was supposed to get my first check. Since then, I had been doing a lot of freelancing, yada, yada, yada.

Irene blew out a whiff of air. "Whew! Sounds like you've been living on faith!"

My first thought was to say, "Well, it doesn't hurt to have a rich best friend, either", but Irene seemed totally serious about this whole faith thing, so I just smiled and nodded because I did not want to go there with her.

When we locked eyes, however, and I knew we were there.

"Tell me about your walk with Christ."

Seeing as Christ and I hadn't crawled together, let alone walked, this was a tough one. I pursed my lips. Shrugged. Nodded. "It's good."

Irene smiled again and pushed my file to the side. She brought an elbow to the table and leaned forward, resting her cheek on her palm. "When and where did you meet Him?"

If I didn't know any better, I'd think she was asking about my new beau. "We met in... a restroom." I could hear Stephanie now: *Oh, that was brilliant, Kerri. You met him in a women's restroom! Which one of you was the cross-dresser?*

Irene's suspicion apparently aroused now, I had to come up with a valid explanation. "I was sick, you see."

"Oh," she sighed. "What was wrong with you?"

Okay, she said *was.* Past tense. I'd had a lot of things wrong with me in the past. Still looking for a way out of this lie, I tried to think of the worst pain I'd ever experienced in my life. I could only come up with, "Strep throat."

"Hmmm," Irene thought aloud for a moment. "I didn't know strep throat was…life-threatening."

"But I also had the flu and an ear infection," I added, stabbing my ear-hole with a finger. "Plus I had pink-eye."

Confused to the point she took off her glasses, Irene asked, "So, your immunity was down?"

I could safely agree to her statement. "Yes. In the past, my immunity was down." Really, who hasn't had a bad Vitamin-C day, a close cousin to the bad hair day?

Irene placed the tip of one stem of her glasses on her bottom lip. Then she began accentuating syllables by striking the air with the entire frame, "So, *you* met *Je*-sus in the *rest*room while your im*mun*ity was down?"

I gave her my best, most innocent smile.

She placed her glasses back on her face and focused her attention on my file again. Irene sighed and eyed the paperwork with lips tucked between her teeth.

I was *losing* her! I couldn't afford to let her slip through my fingers. This was only really job lead I'd had since Stephanie announced her engagement to Ricardo. If I didn't get this gig, I might have to move to a homeless shelter or, worse, move in with my parents.

"Mrs. Trenton," I blurted out as my hands flew into animation mode, "I really need this job. I know I don't have…like…a big story about how I met Jesus. But I *did* meet him in the bathroom, and I *did* say the prayer. And I just…*really, really* need this job." I slumped my shoulders for effect.

Irene closed the folder again and looked me squarely in the eyes. Sincerely. "Kerri, this isn't just a *job*. It's a ministry. I'm not in a position to question your salvation. Only God knows your heart. But I'm not sure your writing skills will make up for the fact that you're so new to the scriptures."

"Well," I scrambled for some ground to stand on, "the job description didn't say how *long* the applicant had to be a Christian."

Irene could only nod in consent. "Yes, but…"

"And it says I have to commit to spiritual growth. I can commit to growing. I mean, I made it to all the way to five foot five," I eagerly offered with my happiest grin.

Irene folded her hands on the desk and laid her eyes dead on mine. This woman must have x-ray soul vision. She was trying to dissect my heart through my eyeballs. It almost hurt! Yet, I couldn't look away. I desperately needed this job like yesterday so I could put up a security deposit and first month's rent at a new place. And maybe, eventually, I could stop driving around in the clunker Stephanie's dad won in a charity gag raffle.

After what seemed like minutes, Irene's face softened and she blinked. "Kerri," she began slowly, "I...can't...exactly tell you why I want to hire you, but I do. I believe you sincerely need a job. I believe you will do anything to get it and that you will indeed grow in Christ in order keep it, which is perhaps the greatest benefit the position has to offer you."

I gave Mrs. Trenton the biggest smile my cheeks could form as she stood to formally give me the green light. "Welcome aboard, Kerri."

"Thank you, Mrs. Trenton. You won't be sorry."

She winked at me. "I know I won't."

Her confidence in me was almost weird. Five minutes ago, I told a chunk of half-truths to her and she figured me out, yet I was still hired to do a job that was, obviously, designed for someone who already knew all this Jesus stuff. I couldn't believe my luck! It had been such a long time since things lined up so well for me.

Seriously, this was the kind of stuff that happened to Stephanie. Like when she met Ricardo in defensive driving class. Who knew that doing the wrong thing – speeding in a school zone, for Pete's sake – would lead to true love?

Mrs. Trenton asked me if I had a few minutes on my hands. Was she kidding? I had all the time in the world. With my consent, she took me on a tour of the department and introduced me to several of my new co-workers.

"Aren't you a sight for sore eyes!" and "What a blessing!" they chirped. A sprightly bunch. Perhaps too sprightly for nine o'clock in the morning.

I wondered if part of this Christian growth thing included a class on how to become a morning person because these people certainly had it together. "Oh, God bless you!" from the man who managed the copy center. "Praise God! I knew He would send just the right person!" from the Media director's secretary. A woman named Mary.

Exactly what was I supposed to say? I would have just smiled, but Mary seemed to want a verbal response. I gave a blank grin and said the only thing that came to mind. "Well, alllllrighty then."

I thought that was clever. Mary did not. She gave Irene a puzzled glance, but Irene didn't acknowledge the silent inquiry. Instead, she led me back to the reception area so I could complete additional paperwork. "Your application says you can start now, correct?"

"Yep. First thing Monday morning," I agreed.

"Actually, you'll need to start Sunday," Irene informed me. "Take notes on the Pastor's sermon and email them to me Sunday afternoon before five o'clock. Our department is responsible for posting summaries of Pastor Scott's message on the website and we've got a pretty quick turnaround time. You can view examples of past sermon notes on the website if you need to get some ideas about format. And, you might want to come to first service at eight o'clock so you'll have more time to write."

Eight o'clock! "Okay," I choked.

I won't lie: I was a totally bummed about having to come to church on Sundays. And at eight o'clock! For all my life, I had known Sunday to be a free day. Sleep late, watch cartoons, eat cereal and keep your pajamas on all day. I couldn't fathom why anyone would forego a lazy Sunday to get up early and get dressed to go listen to somebody talk. How ancient. How unnecessary, especially with the advent of streaming audio.

Mrs. Trenton and I said our good-byes and she left me alone to dot the i's and cross the t's of employment. The receptionist gave me a salary schedule, which dashed all my hopes of getting my own car any time soon. I forgot how little people earned in the non-profit world, precisely why this job was the last on my list.

Once I'd checked all my boxes and signed my name near every X, the receptionist gave me the forms I needed to go take my drug test. Since the results could be expected in 24 hours, she explained, I should be clear to work by Sunday. Next, she gave me my name badge on a bright pink lanyard. "It has a sensor on the back that opens the west doors – where the employees enter."

When I walked out of the church wearing my new name badge, my chest suddenly filled with a warm feeling. I simply labeled it "the gladness of employment."

Chapter 3

Stephanie and I went to a bar to celebrate my "church job" as we called it. Ricardo flew in early that weekend, so I was the third wheel who tried to drink my way beyond my extended awkward presence. As usual, I was unsuccessful. I never actually liked the taste of alcohol, and my mind never actually did the "buzz" thing everyone talked about. The closest I ever got to a "buzz" was a swooning headache. Sometimes, I tried to act drunk to make everyone laugh, but I was always coherent.

Stephanie, however, was an accomplished drinker. She downed several cocktails before taking the dance floor with Ricardo. I sat alone on a stool that would only turn so far one way. Completely annoying. The only thing more bothersome was the string of men who approached me as the night wore on.

"You're a little young to be here, aren't you?" One of them asked between swigs.

"I'm twenty-four," I informed the cowboy hat-wearing stranger who was already wrong for hitting on someone he thought was under age.

He smiled one of those I-haven't-seen-a-dentist-in-years smiles with more space than teeth. My flesh tightened as he took the liberty of rubbing my bare arm. "So, what are you doing here little lady?"

I shirked out of his reach. "I'm having a drink." *Duh!*

"Celebrating something? Your birthday?" he asked.

"No, I'm actually celebrating my new job."

"I've got a"—*belch*— "a new job, too."

I covered my nose. Nothing worse than smelling someone's regurgitated air. "Really, what is your job?" I only wanted to know in case he worked at some restaurant so I could make note to stay clear.

"My new job is pleasin' you," swished between his teeth.

Siiiick! "No, thanks, I'm married."

He tipped his hat. "Then pardon me ma'am. Didn't see the ring."

The 'I'm-married' trick only works on men who actually have an ounce of respect for the institution. The next guy who approached me didn't care about my claim to be married.

"Your husband must be some kind a fool to let a beautiful woman like you out by yo'self." He kept coming back, line after line, until I finally told him to leave me alone.

I was ready to leave, but Stephanie and Ricardo were obviously enjoying themselves too much to step off the hardwoods. I watched them for a while. Her silky hair caught every light, she was curvy in all the right places, and her smile could only be matched by Ricardo's. They were perfect together. Though he wasn't quite the moneybag Stephanie's father probably wanted for her, he was smart and witty. Wouldn't be long before he earned half a million annually trading stocks. That's what was so cool about Stephanie – she saw potential in people.

She had even seen the potential for me to become a Christian. "I don't think it's gonna be that hard," she had encouraged me the night before my interview. "I mean, if you can learn how to deal with your family, you can learn how to be a Christian."

I wasn't quite sure I could do either, actually, but Stephanie's optimism was contagious. She had given me the biggest cheer when I told her got the job. "Woo-hoo! I told you! We've got to celebrate!"

My third suitor of the big celebration night came dressed in black, appropriately. Though he was somewhat attractive – brown locks with a cute set of dimples – he was drunk out of his mind. "I wuzzzthinkin'," he slurred, "mayyyybe we should talk about thisssss."

"About what?" I asked.

"About why you'sss broke up with me."

I shook my head. "I'm sorry. I didn't break up with you. I don't even know you."

He pointed at me and raised his voice, "Yessss, you do!"

"No, I don't."

"Don't lie to me," he cried pitifully, drawing attention to us.

I stepped down from my stool and grabbed my purse. My new employee badge slipped out and fell to the floor.

The man in black beat me to it. He squinted, struggling to read the badge. "What's this? You gotsss a job now?"

"I work at a church," I announced. The bar area fell silent, all eyes averted mine.

That bit of news caught the man in black off guard. He pushed his chin in like a shelf and stared at me. Slowly, he set my name badge on the bar counter. "A church?"

"Yes. A church."

He covered his eyes with one hand. I took the opportunity to retrieve my badge and step away from him.

A moment later, he began sobbing. The bar tender, Lionel, fussed at him, "Mike, you've gotta stop drinking like this." Then he said to me, "Don't worry about him, Miss. Mike's a crying drunk. But if you work at a church, ma'am, you might wanna get outta here."

"I come here all the time."

"Yeah, I've seen you before. I'm just sayin'," he said with a shrug, the meaning of which I didn't understand. "Working at a church and all…"

"Is there something wrong with my being here?"

Lionel finished drying a glass and set it in place before he walked toward me. He leaned over the counter and said quietly, "This place is…not for the likes of you. My old man was a preacher. I think it's pretty safe to say getting drunk isn't really something a church-going woman like you oughta be doing. Makes the Christians look bad, you know?"

Look bad? Why should I care how Christians look? It's not like I was some kind of celebrity whose every move was being scrutinized by the media. There were no holy paparazzi chasing me. As far as I was concerned, what I did in my free time, outside of work, was irrelevant to my job at the church. I wasn't wearing a big Christian sign on my forehead. Besides, who ever said getting drunk was a problem? That wasn't anywhere in the prayer I prayed while I was in the restroom.

Lionel seemed to be waiting for a response. I could only give him a pressed grin, which I suppose he took positively. He winked at me and turned back to his work behind the bar.

I wondered if it was okay for Lionel to be a bartender, since he was a preacher's kid. Then I started wondering about a lot of things – what if people found out I was a Christian? Would they treat me differently? Would they make assumptions about what I should and shouldn't be doing? This whole Christian thing could turn out to be a big, huge problem.

I was going to have to be like my Uncle Edward, who did dirty work for an attorney. Word around the family was that Uncle Edward's boss defended only the guiltiest of criminals; having vital evidence dismissed for stupid but legal reasons, plea-bargaining so violent people could walk the streets again. My mother had confronted Uncle Edward once about his work. He laughed, "You can't have any fun if you let your morals run your life. You have to live a little."

Maybe I could be like Uncle Edward. Christian when I was on the church clock, myself when I was off the clock and out of my co-workers' eyes.

Stephanie and Ricardo finally tired of dancing. Their eyes spoke silent secrets as they approached the bar, arm in arm. "You ready to go?" she asked me.

"Beyond ready," I smiled.

"Aye." Ricardo summoned his Latino heritage to tease me. "Senorita, I saw several men trying to entice you tonight. Surely there was one you would like to get to know better, si?"

Stephanie smiled and nodded in agreement, though she knew I wasn't one to pick up guys at bars.

I shook my head. "No thanks."

Ricardo shrugged his shoulders and looked at Stephanie. "The lady knows what she wants, I see."

"Well, she deserves the best," Stephanie said to me as she hugged my neck with her spare arm. She was definitely tipsy. "It's just a matter of time before the right one comes along."

We walked out of the bar and down Greenville Avenue, which was always crowded on Saturday nights. The sidewalk was lined with couples holding hands and whispering into each other's ears, laughing sweet little laughs.

Ricardo and Stephanie followed behind me in their lovers' waltz. I tried to stay at least four steps ahead of them so they could have their privacy.

The awkwardness was eating me alive. I had to prepare myself for the inevitable. I was losing Stephanie. She would soon be wrapped in the arms of matrimony, enveloped by the cares of wifery. I had, of course, considered these things before. But that night, as we walked back to the car in tricycle wheel formation, it really hit me: I didn't have anyone.

Chapter 4

Sunday morning. My first day on the job. My first time in church since my middle school friend, Valerie, invited me to Vacation Bible School. Even then I had only gone because Valerie told me about the cool door prizes and the food. This was a pattern, I guessed, I only went to church when I needed something.

The parking lot nearest the church was already full, so I had to park across the street at another building. The whole thing reminded me of my junior college campus. Had I known there would be so much walking, I never would have worn my heels.

Stephanie wouldn't call them heels because they were only three inches, but they were heels to me. They went well with my calf-length black skirt and the one-piece imitation button-down-underneath sweater. I'm fully aware that no one is fooled by those, by the way, but it was the most conservative thing I owned next to the interview suit and I didn't want to go to church wearing the same thing. One last peek in my visor's mirror confirmed the truth: the only things I lacked to complete my librarian motif were a hair bun and glasses with a long, dangling chain.

People wearing bright yellow vests guided me to a parking space. With so much traffic, it felt like I was going to a sporting event. I never dreamed so many people went to church. There had to be people from all over the metroplex there—people I encountered at Starbucks and the Department of Motor Vehicles.

I suddenly wondered why no one ever talked about being a Christian or going to church while we were standing in all those long lines talking about nothing in particular. Maybe they were like me. Maybe they only did the Christian thing when they had to.

I joined the masses headed toward the main building where another set of people dressed in fancy suits and dresses guided us into the great room of the church. One of the greeting people gave me a program. Everywhere I looked there was smiling and talking with a light-hearted cheerfulness that reminded me of elementary school, back when everything was possible.

I went with the flow of people and finally found a seat in the center section of the great room, but it would be quite some time before my behind actually met with the cushioned maroon bench. For the next fifteen minutes, everyone stood singing songs and swaying. Though they put the words to the songs up on giant screens, it was clear that almost everyone knew the words by heart. It was actually kind of funny.

The first time I watched the movie *Annie*, I asked my older sister, Natalie, how all those kids who had never seen each other before seemed to know all the words and dance moves to those songs.

"They can read each other's minds because they're all poor. Poor people can do that," she informed me. I wished like crazy I could be poor and obtain the ability to erupt in song and synchronous dance with twenty other kids. I wanted to belong. Crazy thing is – we *were* poor. I just didn't know it at the time.

I did my best to follow along with the words on the screen so I wouldn't stand out like a sore thumb. The beats mixed me up. I made my first professional note to self: *See if we can get that white ball to bounce over the words, like those ridiculously old cartoons, so new members can follow along easier.*

After the media folks showed the words to the songs a few times, the camera crew began capturing live video of the audience. I caught a glimpse of Irene singing and raising her hands. Her eyes were closed. She probably didn't even know the camera was on her. Probably didn't care. She was in complete serenity. I recognized the man next to her from the pictures in her office. Her husband, too, was busy singing blindly.

In the next instant, my face was plastered across the screen! *Oh my gosh! What do I do?* I tried to look away from the camera, wherever it was. Then I tried the next best thing – singing along to a song I had never heard in my life. I swear, I must have looked like a giant fish out of water, gaping *mwa-mwa-mwa.*

But the camera was still on me! I did the only other thing stupid that came to mind. I smiled and gave the camera two thumbs up. The crew quickly took me off screen. An odd murmur bubbled up in the congregation.

That was crazy! Danny never told me about the Orphan-Annie singing and the cameras and the hand-raising and the eye-closing! Good thing Irene wasn't paying attention to the monitors.

By the time we finally sat down, my feet were killing me.

Next, a man stood before the congregation and instructed us to turn to First Corinthians chapter thirteen, verses four through thirteen.

Turn in what?

He continued, "If you don't have your Bibles with you, you may follow along on the screen."

While the crowd listened to him read the information, I wondered if I was going to need a Bible for my job and this Christian thing. When I was in college, there were a few classes I could squeak through without actually buying the book. Hopefully, I could get by without a Bible. And if not, maybe I could just Google it.

The choir followed with a gospel-sounding song that resonated with many members of the audience. Several people stood and clapped along with the choir. It seemed rude to me—I mean, the people sitting behind the standers probably couldn't see. No one seemed to be complaining, though, so I guessed it was okay.

Another man approached the center of the church stage and read off several announcements. This break gave me an opportunity to survey my surroundings in greater depth. There was an elderly couple to my left, a red-headed middle-age man to my right. All ages, races, sizes throughout the building. Some wearing the latest designer fashions, (I know this from watching Stephanie), and some wearing things so old that they were back in style again.

No one really looked like they belonged or didn't belong. Seriously, this place was like…a smorgasbord of people! It was like a big Wal-Mart with singing. *Where did they all come from? Why are they all here? Do they all know each other? How long have they been going to church?*

I started counting rows and people on the rows, but the layout of the building made it impossible to do simple math and come up with a reasonable estimate. There were definitely more than a thousand people there, but not more than two thousand, I guessed. This was only the first service, though. There must have been another thousand or so coming in a few hours. Late sleepers and I couldn't blame them. If it weren't for Irene's deadline, I'd have still been counting sheep.

Following the announcements, the lights dimmed a bit and several people dressed in long, flowing robes took their places. They kind of resembled angels without wings. Soft music played and the dancers, I'd gathered, began to interpret the words with motion. Gently. Lovely. The song was reminiscent of something Nora Jones or Bonnie Raitt might sing, except the chorus was about Jesus; "Precious Jesus," to quote. I liked the way the singer said "Jesus," even though I didn't know what was so special about him.

There was a boy named Jesus in my third grade class. I remember, once, somebody told him he was going to hell because he had a name no one else was supposed to have. But then someone else said he was really good at football, so no one ever raised objection to his name again.

I'd heard people say this special name in fits of anger, almost like swearing. Once, I hissed, "Jesus Christ!" to my sixth-grade classmate for skipping me in the cafeteria line.

I was surprised at the cafeteria lady's reprimand. "Young lady, we don't use God's name in vain here." She stared me down with her cold blue eyes.

I shrank under her glare. With lowered eyelids, I handed her my lunch ticket and whispered, "I didn't even say God, I said Jesus."

"Same thing. Don't you know anything?" She shook her head as she punched a hole in my card.

I stood there, waiting. I thought she was going to tell me what I didn't know, but she didn't. She ordered me to move on, so I did.

Now as I sat in the church listening to the music and watching the dancers grace the stage, I realized that I was just as clueless about Jesus Christ as I was in grade school. And yet, I had been talking to him, oddly enough, in a restroom only a few days ago. Asking him for things. It didn't feel right to ask for things from someone I didn't know, someone I had never given anything to or done anything for.

My enjoyment of the dancing was interrupted by a tapping on my arm. The red-haired man to my right passed me a bucket. The bucket was lined with red fabric and contained checks, envelopes, and cash. *They're giving out money!* I wanted to plunge my hand into the bucket, but I figured it would be rude to take some my first time in church. "Oh, no thanks, I don't need any."

The man squinted his eyes. Then he spoke slowly, as though I might not understand English. "It's for offering, to give." I reached into my pocket, pulled out the change from my morning Starbucks purchase, tossed it into the bucket, and handed it to the older woman to my left.

Offering. Now I remembered. This was the part about religion my father always complained about—giving.

As king of the remote control, my father inevitably stumbled across televangelists here and there. "Baah. All those people want is your money. Pulpit pimps! But there's a fool born every minute to give it to 'em."

I only put a dollar and a few cents in the bucket. I hoped that didn't make me a fool. I also hoped a lot of people would give a whole lot more, seeing as my first paycheck was due in a couple of weeks.

The choir sang another song and then the congregation started fidgeting. Back in high school, we'd all sit around and talk until the bell rang and the teacher walked into the classroom. When she turned on the overhead, we all grabbed our pens and notebooks. Things hadn't changed much because as Pastor Scott approached the podium, people unzipped bags, flipped pages, and apparently prepared to take notes.

Okay, this was crazy. I mean, if there's a church full of people taking notes, why did I have to take notes, too? Why couldn't Irene just copy the notes from someone else? Students do it for each other all the time. Alas, I followed suit. Spiral propped, pen clicked, ready to write.

Pastor Scott prayed first and asked God to use him to bring a word "in season" for us all. He said something about the "sanctuary."

In context, I gathered the sanctuary must be the great room. I always thought a sanctuary was a place where extinct animals were safe, off-limits to hunters and poachers. I rather liked the idea that this church sanctuary was a place where I wouldn't have to worry about attackers. I didn't worry much about being assaulted, but I liked the connotation. *Sanctuary*.

Next, Pastor Scott instructed us to turn to First Corinthians in our Bibles again. I waited for the big screens to show the verse, but they didn't this time. *Great.* How was I supposed to follow the teacher without the book?

I glanced down the row and noticed an official-looking book in one of the wooden pockets. "Excuse me," I disrupted the red-headed man, pointing toward the book, "Could you please pass me that Bible?"

He eyed the book. "That's not a Bible. It's a hymnal."

I sat back. "Oh. Okay."

He reached into the satchel at his feet and handed me another book. "Here, you can use my N-I-V Bible if you'd like."

First of all, what on earth was an N-I-V? Second, who brings a big huge backpack thingy to church? Thirdly, "Thank you," I whispered as I received the book.

He smiled one of those smiles I give to elderly people sitting across from me at the computers in the library when they ask something like, "How do I get to the Internet on this computer, sweetie?" But those people have a generational excuse – they're in their seventies. I, on the other hand, should have known the difference between a Bible and a hymnal.

"Hold your place in First Corinthians for a moment and turn with me to John chapter fifteen," was the next directive from the pastor.

But I just got a Bible! Ugh. Okay. John....J. I flipped the Bible to a spot about halfway through and, surprisingly, found the guidewords "Psalm" at the top. Odd. *Why would a 'P' book be so close to the front of the book?*

I flipped again to the left, still searching for John, and found myself in a state of utter confusion. *Chronicles? Kings? Samuel?* This was sooooo out of alphabetical order.

"When you have it, say amen," from Pastor Scott.

"Amen," from everybody except me.

I stopped flipping through the pages, lest the cameraman find me and prove me a fool again. Pastor Scott read something from this mysterious John book and then everyone flipped back to first Corinthians. In the mass shuffling, I located the table of contents, which confirmed my suspicion that there was no apparent logic to this book's organization.

There was an Old Testament and a New Testament, but they both had old-people names in them. Shouldn't there be a book of Cameron or Kristen? The New Testament should be more new, right?

There were four Johns in the New Testament. I wondered which one Pastor Scott wanted us to turn to—five minutes ago. Panic set in as I realized people were already taking notes. I was so lost in the Bible I'd missed the first part of whatever Pastor Scott said. So I did what I would have done in high school. I asked the lady next me what she had written.

"True love is foreign to the world."

I nodded, writing the words. When I looked up, she wasn't looking back at me. How could she just give me one line? I was certain she had written more than one sentence on her paper.

I tapped her on the shoulder. "Excuse me. What else did he say?"

"He's just expounding on that point."

"Well…what did you write?"

She squinted, shaking her head and shrugging. "They're just some…personal notes."

How can notes *be personal?*

I tried my best to stick with the pastor, but I was totally lost. Worse, he seemed to be talking in this really dreamy mode. The whole thing sounded like a fairy tale. He read a passage about love: love is patient, kind, not rude, on and on and on. I kept thinking: love is impossible. No one I knew was all those things. Stephanie was close, but even she wasn't as perfect as what Pastor Scott talked about.

I wondered if Pastor Scott was all those things. Were all Christians all of those things? This line of thinking brought me to the questions of whether or not *I* could be all those things.

Negative, of course.

The Bible didn't make sense, my notes didn't make sense, and I was starting to wonder if my job didn't make sense. Not to mention the possibility of me being a Christian. Maybe Mrs. Trenton had made a big mistake.

Chapter 5

Stephanie and Ricardo tried their best to help me complete the assignment before five, but we were three blind mice trying to feel our way through a theological maze, over pizza. Ricardo and Stephanie draped across each other on the couch while I sat on the love seat with my toes gripping the edge of the coffee table, laptop perched on my knees.

"Just get on the web," Ricardo finally suggested in desperation. "Maybe you can buy an essay."

I wondered about him sometimes.

Stephanie playfully punched him on the arm. "She can't do that. This is for *church*."

Ricardo shrugged, swallowing his pizza. "She's in a time- crunch. What else is she gonna do?"

"She could ask for more time," Stephanie proposed.

"And look incompetent with her first assignment on her new job?" He blinked rapidly.

"She's *new*. They'll understand."

Ricardo laughed. "In what world? She'll look like a total idiot to her boss."

"She's not an idiot, Ricardo."

I waved from my side of the room. "Hello. I'm right here."

"I didn't say she was – I just said she would *look* like one if she doesn't submit something substantial by five o'clock today." He focused his attention toward me. "You understand me, don't you, Kerri?"

I sighed and nodded, accepting his semi-apology, but I didn't accept his advice.

A true writer at heart, I couldn't turn in someone else's work as my own. I'll admit: I cheated on a calculus exam or two, but never a writing assignment. I had to draw the line somewhere.

4:48 p.m. I withdrew to my bedroom to get down to business. I began drafting the message to Mrs. Trenton, trying a technique I learned in English 101: write what I really want to say first and then edit to make sure I didn't sound like the total idiot both Ricardo and I suspected I was.

Mrs. Trenton,

I'm sorry, but I didn't understand Pastor Scott's message today. I did take some notes, but they're not presentable. I can't make heads or tails of them. For one thing, I didn't know how to navigate the Bible, so I couldn't keep up with the text. I tried to ask the people around me for help, but their notes were, apparently, classified.

I did manage to find the Corinthians and read the stanzas Pastor Scott referenced. My notes are nothing more than questions about those stanzas. No one will benefit from them, so I'd like to keep them to myself for now. Is there a way for me to get a recording of the sermon? Perhaps if I hear the recording, I may be able to make sense of it.

I can only hope that I'll be able to do a better job on future sermons. Will Pastor Scott pick up right where he left off, in the Corinthians, next week? If so, I can go ahead and preview the chapter and, hopefully, things will go better.

Thanks!
Kerri

Now, time to fix up the message. I ran my fingertip along the laptop mouse, centering the pointer over the spell-check button. In a million years, I'll never be able to explain what happened next, but my lunatic fingertip slipped and clicked the "send" button.

"No!"

I watched in horror as the green bar on the bottom of the screen lengthened, signaling the digital transfer. I slammed the escape button. I pressed Control-alt-delete. I battered the Backspace button and the whole keyboard, to which my computer replied, "Message sent."

"Aaaaaaaah!" I screamed.

Stephanie barreled into my bedroom, swinging the door open. "What?"

"I just sent Mrs. Trenton the wrong stupid email message."

"What did it say?"

"Stupid, ignorant, shameful things."

"Like what?"

"Like, I'm a complete nincompoop who doesn't even know how to take notes."

She snarled her face. "Why'd you type that?"

I slammed my palms against my forehead. "I was going to edit it, but I accidentally sent it."

Stephanie's eyes bulged, her mouth stretched wide. "What are you gonna do?"

"I have no idea."

"Ricardo, come here," Stephanie called for help.

For the next five minutes, we tried to retract the message, but my email system couldn't snatch it from Mrs. Trenton's inbox.

"Send her a recall," Stephanie suggested.

"A what?" I queried.

She explained, "Send her a recall message. You know, one that says you'd like to recall your previous email. Haven't you ever gotten one of those?"

"Yeah," I admitted, "but that's kind of like when a judge tells the jury to disregard what they just heard. Like that's gonna happen."

"The jury *has* to forget it, it's the law," Stephanie countered.

I threw myself back on my bed, striking my noggin on my headboard in the process. "Ow! This isn't the law, Stephanie, this is my stupid life!"

Ricardo made a clicking sound with his cheek. "I hate to ask, but do you have any more interviews lined up?"

"Leave." Stephanie pushed him out of my room. "You're not helping right now."

"Honey, I'm just being a realist," he yelled from the other side of the closed door.

Stephanie sat on my bed and tried to give me a pep-talk. It went in one ear and out the other. Actually, I don't even think it went into the one ear. This wasn't like the time I lost two-thirds of my literary analysis paper because I saved it incorrectly. Saving wrong was brainless, yes, but it had a clear remedy. I re-constructed the essay from my notes. In this case, I couldn't take back what I'd already sent.

That's when my next revelation hit me: I was in the real world. The cold, hard world where people who messed up found themselves kicked out onto the cold, hard streets of America. One false flick of the finger and—click!—life as you know it is over.

This was a world where Stephanie's pep-talks didn't work. This was also a world where Stephanie didn't, no *couldn't* live because she always had a family to fall back on. Not just their money and their support, most importantly, their love.

I closed my eyes. "Just leave me alone for a minute."

"Are you sure?"

"Yeah, you'd better go ahead and take Ricardo to the airport."

She relented. "I guess you're right. I'll be back in a few hours. We'll figure out something. Kerri, don't worry, even if you have to stay with me and Ricardo for a few months."

"I couldn't ask you to do that, Stephanie. I can't impose on your newlywed- hood."

She dipped her head down, looking me in the eyes. "I won't be a very *happy* newlywed if my maid of honor is homeless."

I managed a dry smile. "Maybe I'll end up being your maid for life."

"Oh, pulleaze! You'd be like that maid on that old TV show *The Jeffersons*. She never cleaned anything."

"Yeah, I think you're right." I sat up, rising from my position of despair. That's when I noticed Mrs. Trenton's bolded email reply sitting in my inbox.

"Oh my gosh, she's already replied."

Stephanie gasped. "What does it say?

I quickly set my PC on Stephanie's thigh and ordered, "You read it first. If it's good, blink once. Bad, blink twice."

Stephanie focused on the screen now. She clicked the message open. I watched her eyeballs roll from left to right, left to right. Then she stopped and looked at me.

I held my breath as she blinked once. Then she started to blink again but stopped with a squint.

"What's that?" I asked.

"It's a blink and a half."

"What's that supposed to mean?"

"It's both good and bad. She wants you to send your notes and questions anyway."

It was worse than I thought. I threw myself backward on my bed again, bopping my head for a second time. This time, I embraced the pain, which would probably be nothing compared to the ax.

Chapter 6

I left my box of desk décor in the car; wasn't sure if I'd need it given my sermon notes blunder. I was fully prepared to receive a pink slip Monday morning. In fact, I had rehearsed my good-bye speech as I lay awake Sunday night. "I just want to thank all the little people who believed in me. Irene, Stephanie, Lionel the bartender." It sounded more like an academy award-winning actress's speech, but it was fitting since I'd faked my way into the job to begin with.

My heart raced as I waved the magnetized strip in front of the sensors at the west doors. I heard a click—good sign—and the employee door swung open. I was either still employed or the IT guy hadn't gotten the "We fired Kerri Dalee" memo yet. Mrs. Trenton didn't respond to my notes the night before, so I had no idea where I stood.

The office secretary was sitting right where I'd seen her last, and it seemed her bangs had slipped into the exact same spot. She flipped them back again. "Good morning, Kerri."

Did she know something I didn't know? I couldn't be sure. I barely lifted my hand to wave. "Good morning."

"You remember the way to your desk?"

"Yes, thank you."

She buzzed me in and wished me well on my first full day. *We'll see.*

I made eye contact with no one as I rounded the corners to my cubicle. I could have been an overgrown mouse, I was so quiet. There were a few "hellos" directed at me, but nothing to alert security.

I had my cubicle in sight when Irene blindsided me with, "Morning, Kerri." Her face was as cheerful as the first time I laid eyes on her. She wasn't fuming, she wasn't clinching her teeth. She was just...Mrs. Trenton.

"Good morning."

She pointed toward my desk. "I put a rough draft of the sermon notes on your desk. I need you to copyedit and get it back to me ASAP so we can post by ten o'clock."

Was this the twilight zone? Irene acted as though nothing had happened, like I hadn't emailed that crazy message the night before. Maybe this was like the day before my old company announced its bankruptcy. Upper management must have known it was our last day of operation, but they carried on with business as usual—probably so the employees wouldn't do the whole riot and loot thing. Nonetheless, they knew, and they had allowed the rest of us to walk around in oblivion.

The anxiety was killing me. *I have to know.* "Irene, what about...you know...the email I sent you last night?"

"Your notes were great," she said. "I put the answers and Biblical references regarding your questions on your desk. Your questions actually helped me refine the notes so that anyone, a new Christian or one who's been in the faith for a while, can understand Pastor's message."

I glanced at the printout of my email lying on my desk, with handwritten notes beside each one. This was worse than flunking a test. She actually expected me to study the *correct* answers. I hated having teachers like that! I much preferred the low grade with a crossword puzzle for extra credit grading plan.

"And I also got you some Bible tabs. They're here, on your seat." She took the liberty of stepping into my cubicle. Irene held up the gold tabs with black lettering. "You just take your Bible and stick these tabs onto the first pages of each book. They'll help you locate the books easily."

I was going to have to get a Bible after all. Maybe even the Bible cliff notes, too.

"I'll leave you to your editing." She handed me the Bible tabs. "And don't forget these."

"Oh, thanks." I searched her eyes again for a hint of hirer's remorse and saw none. "I'll put these on my Bible as soon as…" the words 'I get home' would have made the perfect lie. Probably wouldn't have raised an eyebrow. But somehow the option to lie escaped me; erased by Irene's kindness. I finished my thought with, "as soon as I get one." I lowered my eyes to the ground and my behind into my chair.

Irene softly asked, "Do you need a Bible, Kerri?"

In desperation, I confessed, "I need, like, everything, Irene. I need to know what I'm supposed to do with all this Christian stuff. I need to know how much it's going to affect my life. Like, what to do and what not to do. By the way, can I drink?"

She shrugged, "You can do anything you want to do. The only question is how it will affect your walk with Christ."

"Walk *where*? I mean all this stuff is like…Luke Skywalker, the Twilight Zone and Harry Potter rolled into one. It's not *real* to me."

Irene smiled and shook her head. Her features softened. "That's the most *real* thing I've heard from anybody in a long time.

"And let me tell you Kerri, there are, sadly, many Christians who have been in church for a long time but still don't know Christ through their own, personal experience. Understanding that you need to know Christ is profound in itself."

Not helping.

"Why don't you go ahead and head over to H-R. They've got a few things they need you to do. Then you can get to the editing. I'm sure the church has a Bible I can give you. Check back with me later today." She winked at me and then exited my enclosed office space.

She must really think I'm crazy now. If I were my boss, there's no way I'd keep me around. Irene was amazing. I didn't know why she was putting up with me, but I was sure glad for it.

And what's with all this winking?

My first in-office morning at my new job flowed smoothly. I went to the human resources office to watch a few orientation videos. Then I spent another hour working with the technology folks to get my computer password, e-mail account, phone, and fax line established. The technician kept assuring me that the process usually didn't take as long as it was taking for me to get set up in the system.

I played along with his light chatter . "Pretty much the story of my life – I'm a little slower sometimes."

"Naaaa. It's not you. The system is just slow today for some reason."

Sounded like something Stephanie would say— something positive to keep me from degrading myself.

I stayed on hold for quite some time before Mr. IT was finally able to give me my professional contact information. "Thanks."

"You're welcome. I'll go ahead and forward this info to human resources. They should have your business cards printed by the end of the week."

I thanked him again.

The thought of my name front and center on a business card created some degree of enthusiasm. Now I could register for weekly free lunch drawings at local restaurants. I could also use the cards to pick chicken from between my teeth with ease. Really, what else was I going to do with them? I couldn't actually give them to anybody, not after the way the people at the bar reacted.

Picture it: the man of my dreams is coming down an escalator. I'm going up. Briefly, we lock eyes. He waves hello. I mouth it back. In an instant, we both realize it's love at first sight, but we've passed each other now. He's running back up the escalator, I'm running down. People feel the magic and move aside so we can be across from each other. He asks me for my number. I whip out my church card. He studies it, looks at me in bewilderment—like he never knew me. He stumbles, tumbles down the escalator, bumps his head and gets amnesia. Just like that, my almost-husband forgets he ever loved me.

No. I would not let this tragedy happen to me.

I finished the copyediting and walked the article back to Irene's desk before eleven. If I couldn't be accurate, I could at least be timely. "Here you go."

"Great." She eyed my comments. "Looks good."

She might as well have put a gold star next to my name. "I'm glad you like it."

"I'll make the changes in my file and send it to the webmaster now. This should go by much quicker next week when your email is up and running. Has technology set up your account yet?"

"Yeah, they just finished."

She nodded and reached into her desk. "I got a Bible for you."

This Bible was much heavier than the N-I-V the stranger had shared with me during Sunday service. I had to wonder, though, why one Bible would be so much thicker than another one if they all contained the same information. This wholr mystery was beyond me.

"Thank you." I accepted the Bible and headed back to my cubicle for a cram session.

Chapter 7

I was in the swing of things toward the end of the week. I'd learned that you could pretty much respond to anything with some form of the word "bless" and be okay. If Audra, the main receptionist, asked how I was, I replied, "Blessed." If Pike from the mailroom shared good news, I should comment, "What a blessing." And if I wanted to say something bad about someone, I should I concluded my commentary with, "Bless her heart." Mary taught me that one as I listened to her talk to another secretary one day in the break room.

Stephanie said I should make a diary of my first week. "It would be cool. The secret life of church people."

We sat in Starbucks enjoying one of our favorite past times, downing coffees and cakes. No real food, just an evening of carbs and caffeine. I wondered if we would still be able to have our Starbucks nights after she married Ricardo. I also wondered how much longer our metabolisms would allow us to eat whatever we wanted without gaining a pound. My mother always said the Dalee women were thin until we hit forty, "But after that, everything shifts to the front."

A steady flow of java seekers streamed through the store. Invariably, the hot guys gave Stephanie a second glance. When her huge engagement ring dashed their hopes, they gave me the once-over, probably wondered how young I was, and then decided I wasn't worth investigating. The whole routine took no more than ten seconds. Stephanie was oblivious to the silent auction.

She slurped happily, discussing the latest with the upcoming wedding. "The planner is freaking out because Ricardo's cousin, you know, the flower girl?"

I nodded.

"Well, she's hit this mad growth spurt and she keeps getting taller. When the time comes, we'll have to make adjustments to her dress at the last minute.

I took a sip of my Terraza blend, and then asked a few obligatory questions. How's the catering coming along? What about the music? I listened to her answers, shifting my eyes between my cup and Stephanie's lips. She rambled off a few more details and finally announced that she was tired of talking about the wedding because the whole thing fried her nerves. She didn't want to spend the rest of the year frazzled.

Ditto.

She switched the subject. "So, how was work today? Meet any hot guys?"

"There are no hot guys at my job."

Stephanie clapped rapidly. "Stop that! There are hot guys everywhere. You just have to look for them."

"If they were truly hot, wouldn't it be obvious?"

"No, no, no! Absolutely not." Stephanie shook her head. "There is such a thing as hidden hotness."

"And exactly how am I supposed to recognize this hidden hotness?"

"You just gotta watch out for it. Sometimes it hits you when you least expect it. Could be the custodian, you never know." With anyone else, I might have laughed. But Stephanie was serious. She dated the pizza delivery guy for a while because he was nice, ambitious, and especially prompt.

"I'll turn on my hot-o-meter next week. Right now, I'm just trying to survive. Everyone there knows, like, everything about everything about God and I'm just now getting to Noah's Ark."

"I've heard about Noah's ark. That's a good place to be. Isn't it?"

"Yeah, if you like animals, I guess."

We finished our carbs and left the restaurant in total jitters. It probably should have been illegal to consume so many empty calories in one sitting. Awesome.

The smell of our un-emptied trash met us at the door when we returned to our apartment. I apologized to Stephanie for not taking holding up my end of the chores. "I've gotta get my morning routine together."

While I busied myself with the garbage, Stephanie checked the voice messages. "Your mom called."

I sat the offending black plastic bag on the porch and mentally blocked out Stephanie's announcement. Maybe if I clicked my heels three times, this wouldn't be happening. "What did she say?"

"Someone died. One of your aunts. She wants you home for the funeral."

My chest thumped heavily as a blanket of anxiety covered me. Not because I'd had one of those life-changing moments where you suddenly realize how important your family is, but because I really didn't *care* who'd died. "Erase the message."

"I will not erase it!"

"I'm not going."

Suddenly, Stephanie was on me like white on rice. "You can't keep running away from your family, Kerri."

I blamed Stephanie's dad for insisting on a landline with old-fashioned communal voicemail.

"I'm not running away from them. I'm just...jogging away."

"You know what?" Stephanie put both hands on my shoulders and forced eye contact. "You've got what it takes to stand up to them now. You have a job, you have security, and you're a Christian. You're, like, a whole new person."

"You gonna send the big, 'Kerri isn't a loser', note to my family?"

"They won't need a note. They'll have *you* standing right in front of them. Flash your name badge, you know?"

I turned my back to her and walked toward the bathroom. "I'm not going."

Stephanie followed me and stood there watching me wash my hands four times. "Clean enough?"

Tears began to sting my eyes as I turned off the faucet and wiped my hands on a towel. Stephanie couldn't understand that life wasn't so easy. How could she? She was rich and spoiled by her family – in a good way. Not the bratty, look-what-I-have-that-you-don't kind. She was the have-one-of-mine type. I'm thinking a person can only be so generous when they have more than enough of everything, including love.

"I can't go. Drop it, okay?"

She held up her hands out, palms facing me. "Let me just say this one thing."

I crossed my arms. "Shoot."

"God forbid this to happen," she began. "But what if...I don't know...what if you need a transplant? What if whatever happened to the dead person in your family is hereditary and you have this disease and the only way you can live is to get an organ from your family?"

I could only laugh at her hypothetical scenario. "Trust me. If I'm ever in a position where my family is the only entity that can help me, I'm as good as dead already."

The phone rang again. Stephanie grabbed it from my bed before I could look at the caller ID. "Hello? Yes. She's right here." Stephanie mouthed *it's your mom*.

I shook my head, pushed the phone away. Stephanie pushed back. We very nearly played a game of hot-potato with the phone.

I heard my mom yelling, "Hello? Is anyone there?"

The child in me stood at attention as the phone fell to the floor. Stephanie picked it up, placed it in my hand, and shoved it to my ear.

"Kerri?"

My stupid breathing must have given me away. "Yes."

"I haven't heard from you in ages. You *do* have a mother, you know?"

Stephanie abandoned me. My tongue failed me. *God, help me.* "H-hello, Mother."

"Did you get my message? Your Aunt Flora died Wednesday. We're having the funeral Saturday."

"Oh. Okay," was all I could muster. Aunt Flora was the last of my father's siblings. Maybe now that she was gone, I could rest around the Dalee's again.

"Aren't you coming?"

Do guppies go to shark funerals? Would hyena go to a lion's funeral? "No."

My mother huffed. "You're gonna break your Grandma Dale's heart."

"Grandma Dalee is dead."

"That's what makes it even worse."

A chuckle escaped my throat and chaos came barreling through the receiver. "Haven't you learned anything over all these years? Respect your elders! You'd think after all this time and all the trouble you caused by not obeying this one simple rule, I swear! They say the middle child is always the worst and I do believe they're right!"

The six years I'd put between myself and my family suddenly rewound. It was like my mother had this mental time machine and she always took me back to this one horrible era.

"I'll send flowers."

"Kerri Ann Dalee you will *not* send flowers, you will *bring* yourself home and spend time with your family. It's the least you could do after all that happened. Your Aunt Flora was always your favorite aunt before, well, you know."

"Can you say it?"

My mother gasped. "Say what?"

I stopped for a moment, waited for the words. "Can you just, for once, say what happened?"

"There's no need for me or anyone else to repeat what happened. It's over."

I blew a frustrated sigh. "I'm not coming to the funeral."

"Then I won't be coming to your wedding."

"What wedding?"

Her voice dropped an octave. "You can't live with Stephanie forever. It doesn't look right, two grown women living together, if you know what I mean. People are starting to ask questions about you."

She was making me seriously crazy. "I have to go."

"Your brother is driving in from Houston Friday evening. He says he can pick you up on the way in and drop you off in Dallas on the way back. He's only staying one night." She had given this some thought. "Call him if you change your mind."

"I'm not going to change mind," I assured her.

"Neither will I."

Chapter 8

Friday night at seven o'clock on the dot, there was a knock at the door. Stephanie was expecting Ricardo, so she hopped from the couch and rushed toward the door, sliding the last few feet on her socks. For safety's sake, she looked through the peephole. "Who is it?"

"Britt."

Britt? I stormed to the door. *I never gave my brother my address.*

Stephanie let him in and there before me was a face I hadn't seen in the two years since my father's triple bypass surgery. My heart dropped to the floor, but I couldn't let myself cry. I had to remember: I was angry. Very angry. How dare he come pick me up after I'd made it clear to our mother that I was not going to the funeral?

Stephanie shrieked for us. "So, are you two just gonna stand there or what?"

My older brother opened his arms and I cautiously scooted into them. I inhaled the scent of his cologne. He hadn't changed brands. The familiarity was almost overwhelming.

I blinked back tears and put on my game face as he released me from his embrace. "What are you doing here, Britt?"

His lips turned down at the corners while he shrugged. "I thought you wanted to ride with me to Oklahoma."

"Let me guess. Mother told you this, correct?"

Britt threw his head back. "Something told me to call you first. I'm really sorry, Kerri. I should have known. But I don't have your number. Mom gave me your address, told me to pick you up on my way from Houston."

"Oh my gosh! You two haven't seen each other in, like, forever!" Stephanie pulled us into a group hug. "This is amazing!"

"No, this is a big mistake," Britt agreed with me.

"No way," Stephanie dismissed his comment. "Seeing family is never a mistake."

I raised an eyebrow. "Depends on whose family you're talking about."

Britt eyed me and nodded. "Truly."

Then there came another knock on the door. This time it was Ricardo, bearing flowers for Stephanie. She took the bouquet, wrapped her arms around Ricardo's neck and kissed him for dear life. Between pecks, she introduced Ricardo to Britt.

While the lovers finished their "hello" smooching, Britt and I took seats in the living room across from each other. I sat down, warming my usual spot on the love seat while Britt sat in the chair.

My brother and I were both cursed with unnatural thinness. I suppose it was more a curse for him, being a guy, than it was for me. Dad always said Britt and I would be the first to go if the depression ever hit again. When we were kids, Britt, our sister Natalie, and I used to have secret eating contests. We'd eat until it literally hurt. Britt always won the contest, but he never gained an ounce.

At six foot one now, he could have used another 30 pounds. He tried to obscure his slight build by wearing an undershirt, but his bony shoulders still gave him away.

"You could use a good meal, aye?" I teased, repeating one of our father's favorite lines.

He grinned. "I haven't heard that one in a while."

"Yeah, I know."

We sat there looking at each other for a moment. His brown hair matched by mine, the eyes and noses nearly exact duplicates. And yet, for all we had in common, we were strangers. The sadness of this reality almost came seeping out of my eyes so I quickly grabbed the remote control and engaged in a game of channel surfing.

Britt must have felt it, too. He fidgeted for a moment, checked his watch twice. "What have you been up to?"

"Not much."

"Same here," he said.

"I'm sorry you wasted your time coming here. I'm not going to the funeral. But it was good to see you again, I guess."

"Same here. No problem, I needed to stretch my legs anyway." Britt had mastered the fine art of separating himself from all emotion a long, long time ago. I couldn't blame him, though. I sometimes wished I had mastered it to protect myself from our family.

Ricardo and Stephanie joined us in the living room, relieving our awkward stress but creating another thorny situation. Stephanie threw herself across Ricardo's lap while his hand lay high on her thigh. They looked like a couple of teenagers on their first unsupervised date. Way too much public affection. Times like this, I wished they would just take it to Stephanie's bedroom.

"You two look like twins, I swear," Stephanie remarked.

Nothing Britt and I hadn't heard before. We were four years apart in age, but the more time passed, the gap seemed to cinch such that, starting with our twenties, we looked as though we could have the same birthday. Too bad our relationship didn't get closer with time.

Ricardo nudged his nose beneath Stephanie's earlobe. She giggled and told him to behave. "We've got company."

He whispered something into her ear and she blushed softly. I couldn't help but be embarrassed.

Britt fixed his eyes on the television screen.

Finally, Stephanie pulled Ricardo from the couch by an arm. "Have a safe trip to Oklahoma. It was nice seeing you again, Britt."

"Likewise." Britt stood, tugging his pants back in place.

Stephanie wrapped Ricardo's arms around her waist. She asked me, "Maybe you could stop back by on your way back to Houston Sunday? We could all do brunch after Kerri and I come back from church."

Ricardo posted the time-out signal. "Whoa-whoa-whoa, who's going to church?"

"Oh, Babe, Kerri and I going to church so I can help her take notes."

Ricardo's eyes rolled toward the ceiling and back down to Stephanie again. "Babe, you don't go to *church*. I mean, that's not really what we *do* when I come to town."

She bristled slightly and wagged her head in defiance. "I'll have you know, I did go to church a few times when I was a kid. My grandmother was active."

"It's just for a few hours. I'll have her back before eleven – before you ever get out of bed. Scout's honor." I crossed thumb over pinky and held my three middle fingers straight, believing I had addressed his concern adequately.

Ricardo squinted his eyes, dumbfounded. "Church is for brainwashed...dreamers."

My stomach tightened. *Did he just say that?*

Britt chimed in. "We never went to church when we were younger. What gives, Kerri?"

I tackled the easiest first. "I *work* at a church, okay?"

Now for Ricardo. "Church is not just for losers." That didn't come out right. I added, "Lots of regular people go to church. Normal, decent people who know how to think for themselves and like to look on the bright side of things."

"No offense, Kerri, but you're not the most focused, purposeful person on the planet. This whole church thing could be another fleeting obsession. You and Stephanie are good at those, you know?" A condescending smirk slinked across Ricardo's face.

I was forced to acknowledge the truth of his statement. In the eighteen months he had been dating Stephanie, I'd done nothing more than flutter from job to job, career to career, dream to dream.

My shoulders slumped in defeat. Maybe he was right.

Stephanie intervened. "Stop it. It's just *church*." She swiveled, set her chest against his, then tip-toed for a kiss.

His body relented. "Well, I really don't want you to go – at least not while I'm here. We rarely get to see each other as it is, Stephanie."

She whined, "Yeah, I know, babe." Then she cast an apologetic glance at me. "I'm sorry, Kerri. Ricardo's got a point. I'll go with you next Sunday while he's in Florida."

And there it was again – the slow and painful loss of my best friend. I really liked Ricardo, I just hated him for taking Stephanie away from me. My heart made some loud, painful thuds in my chest as I swallowed to keep the lump in my throat at bay.

"Kerri, why don't you…just…go to the funeral with your brother?" Ricardo made the worst suggestion possible.

Britt stood, swiped his pants. "I could use the company."

Stephanie's lips moved and she almost said something, but she stopped, pursed her lips, awaiting my response.

Clearly, it was three against one. And staying with those two would be miserable. Perhaps even hostile. Not much different than what I could expect if I hopped in the car and rode to Oklahoma with Britt which, at that point, was probably the lesser of two evils.

Okay, Dalee family, here I come.

Chapter 9

One call to Irene garnered a ton of sympathy and the opportunity to stay home from work Monday to recuperate. I took the sympathy but declined the day off. For one thing, I hadn't built up any vacation time. I couldn't afford to be docked. Secondly, it just didn't feel right missing a day of work in the second week. Probably wouldn't look good on my 90-day review.

My work arrangements taken care of and my attitude thoroughly awful, I hopped into the passenger's side of Britt's SUV. He really tried to make the trip bearable by posing silly questions only a stranger would ask. I was in no mood for chit-chat. It took him a while to get the hint, but he finally ramped up his satellite radio and soothed our trip with uninterrupted 90's hits.

I pouted internally the whole way. There I was at odds with my best friend's fiancé, about to step into a nightmarish flashback with faces I hadn't seen since I drew a line in my life's sand.

These people, my family, had forsaken me on so many levels I'd lost count. My extended family refused to come to my junior college graduation because they thought I should have used my Pell Grant money to pay for Grandpa Dalee's funeral. Thank God I was legally old enough to make that decision for myself.

Even closer relatives were jealous because we lived in a partially-bricked house, thanks to my dad's attempt to modernize the 1930-something shack. Not to mention the unmentionable rift between Aunt Flora and my father on account of me.

Britt helped me unload my suitcase from the back of his vehicle. Together, we walked the few steps from the dirt driveway to my parents' home in Crookshaw, Oklahoma. Everything was just as I remembered it; dirty red brick with peeling white border and crooked, broken steps leading to the porch. Even the sideways doorbell hadn't been repaired.

To the best of my knowledge, the reason we lived in such an old house was because my great-grandfather willed it to my father, an act which heaped drama on top of drama with the family. This "free house" often referenced in many a drunken family argument was one of the reasons my parents were able to send me to a junior college. My sister, Natalie, had no desire to go to college, and Britt went into the military. Meanwhile, most of my cousins were lucky to finish high school.

"I suppose we'd have money, too, if we didn't have to pay rent," I'd heard my Aunt Myrna say.

"Look at him – got a kid in college, sitting like a fat cat," I'd heard my Great Uncle Barney whisper.

I braced myself for the onslaught of existing bad memories and future bad memories waiting to be birthed this weekend.

Britt knocked on the door and almost immediately my mother answered. "Oh, I'm so glad you made it!" As she embraced him, I could only see her hands pressing into his back. My mother wore long, oval-shaped acrylic nails. They were definitely a step up from the press-ons she super-glued onto her abused finger nubs since the mid-80's. I could also see an abundance of wrinkles and light liver spots on her hands. Had that much time passed since I saw her last?

She released Britt and then it was my turn. She crossed her arms. "Kerri! Oh my goodness, look at you. You're so skinny!"

If I didn't have any manners, I would have told her that she wasn't looking so hot, either. Just like Aunt Flora had advised, my mom's skin, eyes, and hair bore the telltale signs of a longtime smoker. And, just as mom warned, everything had indeed shifted to the front.

I sucked up her insult and crossed the threshold, returning her brief hugging gesture and inhaling the indelible smell of cigarette smoke spilling out of the house. Already I wondered how long it would take to get the odor out of my clothes. "Hello, Mother."

She held me at arm's length. "You don't look well. Are you sick?" She gasped, putting a hand over her mouth. "Oh my gosh."

Next thing I knew, she was pressing my chest with two fingers. "Are you doing your self-exams?"

I shooed her hand away. "Mother, you cannot do a *self*-exam on *someone else's* breasts!"

She warned, "Well, you know cancer runs in our family."

"*Smoking* runs in our family, mom, not cancer. And, no, I'm not sick."

She peered into my eyes. "Are you on drugs?"

"No, but right now they don't sound too bad."

She tilted her head and peered down her nose at me. "Hmph."

"I'm only kidding, Mother. I'm fine, okay? I'm as skinny as I've always been. Not one pound more or less."

"Well, come on in, sweetheart. Your father's in the den."

Let the second phase of torture begin.

As I made my way down the long hall of photographs lining the main walkway of the home I knew as a teenager, I couldn't help but scrutinize this wall of memories. There was a giggling kindergarten picture and a first grade wide, snaggle-toothed grin. A lopsided ponytail in second grade, but my teeth were growing in nicely. Big

teeth in third grade all the way through sixth grade. I "lost" the picture order forms for my middle school years, thanks to zits. I couldn't escape the classic senior cap-and-gown picture, which so accurately documented my battle with acne because my parents wouldn't pay the extra fifteen dollars to have them airbrush me. Fifteen dollars was a decent chunk of money to us. Yet and still, I'd seen them spend a small fortune on cigarettes.

"You want to remember yourself for what you are, Kerri," my mom had argued as she sealed the picture envelope only with the minimum payment enclosed. "You have pimples, alright? Maybe in another twenty years you'll be a beautiful swan, but right now you're an ugly duckling. You can't change the facts."

Sadness gripped my chest and threatened to come spilling out of my eyes. I had to pull myself together. If I couldn't make it through the first ten minutes, how was I going to make it through the next twenty-four hours?

I took a detour off the hallway and headed for my old bedroom instead of the den. I wasn't ready to face my father just yet. He was asleep anyway.

The unmistakable sound of his snoring—like elephants on steroids charging through the jungle—made the house rattle. Somehow, we had all managed to live through this resounding nuisance. We ate through it, read through it, watched television through it, slept through it like white noise.

I slipped into my old room and closed the door behind me. With my back to the hard wall, I took a series of deep breaths. I tried to tell myself over and over: *It's not that bad, Kerri. You can do this.* But the deep breaths began bordering hyperventilation. *Oh, great. That's the last thing I need right now.* I closed my eyes and tried to imagine something peaceful; a quiet beach, Bambi, two Benadryl capsules.

And then, from somewhere in the newly formed recesses of my church-job mind, I remembered something Irene wrote in response to one of my questions: *When you don't know what to do, pray to God. He won't leave you without help.*

I didn't know exactly how or what to ask God, but I knew I needed something to help me get through my family. I took two steps, dropped my knees on the 70's staple braided oval rug, and folded my hands in prayer the way I'd seen a picture of some guy named Daniel praying in my Bible. He was surrounded by lions. Very fitting.

God,

Ummmm...I don't know if you do things to people's families, but if you do, could you please do something to mine? Make them regular, I guess? I don't mean regular like going to the bathroom regular. Oh! I'm sorry. That was gross. And you already knew what I meant.

I stopped praying, gathered my thoughts and pushed on.

Okay, God, I'm back.

If making them normal is too much to ask, could you at least make me strong enough to handle them? I think that's better, probably, because it may be easier to fix just me than fix all of them. Okay, so that's the plan: fix me, and maybe I can ignore them a little better. Maybe you could stuff my ears with, like, super-absorbent supernatural cotton balls. Alright? Thank you.

I pushed off my bed, but quickly allowed myself to drop back down.

Oh! I almost forgot. In Jesus' name I pray, Amen.

No sooner than I finished the prayer, my mother burst into the room. Like a startled child who'd been caught jumping on the bed, I froze.

"What are you doing?"

I rose from the floor and stood for a moment, wringing my hands. "Praying."

"*Praying?* You *are* sick, aren't you? I knew it!"

"I'm not sick. I'm just praying because…I think I need to."

My mother squint her eyes and stepped toward me. She put her hand on my forehead. Then she called out to my father. "Sam!"

After a few more tries, he finally answered, "Eh?"

"Get up, you lazy slop! Come see what's wrong with your daughter - she's praying."

"She's *what*?" A semi-concerned tone painted his voice.

My mother finally relinquished my forehead so that she could open the bedroom door wider and yell down the hallway. "Praying!"

"What for?"

My father shuffled toward my bedroom. His ever-present plaid shirt and khaki work pants with reinforced knees had not changed. But, like my mother, he was aging. Every feature on his face seemed to have slipped an inch, plus he'd lost another inch of his hairline.

"Hey."

"Hello, Dad."

He hacked a few times. "What're you praying for?"

I shrugged. "For strength, for life."

He slung a haphazard wave. "Prayer is for idiots too lazy to figure things out for themselves. You're not an idiot, are you?"

Gulp. "No. I'm not an idiot, Dad, I'm a Christian."

He mumbled, "Even worse."

Chapter 10

Any normal bereaved family would spend their time reflecting on precious memories of the deceased. Not mine. By the time Natalie joined the funeral, word had spread around the family that I was a Christian. Now there was another reason for everyone to despise me.

I tried to shake the feeling that I was being scrutinized. Maybe it was all in my head. Maybe I was just being egotistical. Or maybe I was just exhausted from lack of sleep on top of the drive from Dallas. *They couldn't all be thinking about me.*

Sitting on the eighth row in the funeral home, Natalie cornered me. "So what's up with the Christian stuff?"

I gave her the same snotty smile I'd given her since we were kids. Natalie was only eleven months younger than me. By all accounts, we were inseparable as preschoolers. Somewhere around third grade, someone stamped "Special Education" on Natalie's manila life-folder and everything changed for her. She withdrew into her art—mostly crayon drawings. Later, she painted beautiful watercolor landscapes that lived forever under her bed.

She was diagnosed dyslexic, but by then it was too late. She hated school, hated people—mostly herself.

Seeing as we were sitting right next to each other, I had to answer her question. "I accepted Christ as my savior."

"When? Where? Why?"

An elderly cousin whom I vaguely recognized looked back at Natalie and me to let us know we were talking too loudly.

I pulled my best ventriloquist act. "Last week. In the restroom, I needed a job."

Natalie shook her head and whispered, "Well, keep it to yourself. Mom's freaking out. She says you're trying to find yourself and she hopes you're not on drugs."

The cousin turned around this time and shushed us with an index finger to her lips.

Natalie stuck out her tongue. I hadn't seen that one in a long time, which caused an uncontrollable giggle to escape my grasp. Now, several rows of Daylee's turned to give us both evil eyes. They were, of course, right to express their objections, but I really couldn't help it. Sometimes it is physically impossible to stop laughter.

When we were little, Natalie always made me laugh. She'd make funny faces and sing crazy songs about stinky feet. Mother always said Natalie was a lost cause, so silly and busy with her art.

"You definitely got your crazy brain from your mom's side of the family," my dad would tell her.

Now as we sat shoulder-to-shoulder in the dank parlor of what had to be the smallest, cheapest funeral home in the county, Natalie and I clasped hands to help contain ourselves.

I kept my eyes forward, absorbing the few words of comfort spoken to our family and admiring the floral arrangements that I figured the funeral home must provide whenever the deceased didn't have enough.

For a moment, I tricked myself into thinking maybe I'd been wrong about my family. Maybe we weren't polar opposites of Stephanie's family. Maybe we didn't belong on our own reality show. Then I had to remind myself that Natalie and I always got along for the first ten minutes.

I'd managed to lay fairly low at the burial. I stuck by the ever-cold Britt's side and nodded at a few faces. I'd packed Stephanie's least fashionable black dress. Although I'd draped the dress with a cashmere cardigan, no one in my family was familiar enough with cashmere to suspect how much the ensemble cost. Rayon might have given me away, but not cashmere.

Apparently, someone in town got word about Aunt Flora's death and convinced a church's hospitality team to bring a few covered dishes to Aunt Flora's house. My dad made a joke about the church folk feeding us with long-handled spoons. His comment signaled opening day on me.

Natalie fired the first shot. "Hey! Quiet everyone! Quiet!" As soon as the house hushed, my sister continued, "It's true. Kerri is a Christian now. She wants to say grace over the food!" She bit her thumbnail. The corners of her lips coiled into a sinister grin.

Well, so much for sisterly bonding. In an instant, roughly thirty people—far more than the Fire Marshall would recommend gathering in Aunt Flora's small frame home—stopped and stared at me. The heat from the spotlight caused me to sweat.

"Go ahead, Kerri," My father teased. "Pray, little Miss Christian."

"How can she be a Christian after she took the money we needed for Grandpa's funeral?" came from between my Cousin Amanda's clinched teeth. Mind you, I don't even think Amanda was old enough to remember the man's life or death. This was urban legend for as much as she knew.

"And after what she accused my father of doing," Lance, the oldest and meanest of Aunt Flora's three children whined. "I'd sooner let the devil pray over my food than her. She drove my mom to an early grave, if you ask me." He burst into tears, threw his beer mug against a wall, sending slivers of glass into my step-uncle Hugh's arm.

"Dadgumit, Lance! You cut me!" Uncle Hugh hollered, plucking a piece of glass from deep within his arm.

Uncle Hugh grabbed Lance by the collar and the two of them began tussling while other family members tried to pull them apart. It was wild, I tell you. And no one was even drunk yet.

Britt whisked me out the front door before they had a chance to remember who'd started this rumble. As we trudged across the bare front yard, past the chained-up pit bull puppy nipping at our heels, Britt pulled his key fob from his pocket. "Let's get out of here, Kerri."

My mother came barreling behind us. "Wait! Where are you two going?"

Britt stopped in his tracks and pivoted back to face her. "We're going home, mom. This family is nuts."

"We ain't *all* nutty," she said, eyeing me.

"Mom, I'm not crazy. I'm a Christian," I stated.

She crossed her arms. "There's nothing wrong with you believing in God. But you come in here praying and highfalutin in front of everybody, what'd you expect to happen, Kerri?"

"I was praying to *God*! And what on earth did I falute highly?"

"Well," she shook her head, "you've got your church job and your church sent that big 'ole plant setting at the front of the funeral parlor. It was right up there next to the one Stephanie sent, God knows her plant could take up a hearse all by itself. Plus, I heard your church sent a resolution to the funeral home and everything, in support of the family of *Karee Dalee* and so on. It's like you're a card-carrying Christian, come to make us all look heathens, on top of your college degree and all."

I should have known Stephanie would send something extravagant. But I thought Irene was asking all those questions about the funeral in order to make sure I wasn't skipping out on work. I hadn't realized she was determining where to have flowers delivered.

"Why did you insist on me coming back, Mom? You've done nothing but belittle me since we got here."

She looked into the sky and snubbed her nose at me. "I was just hopin' maybe with Aunt Flora dyin', you could apologize finally and get things back to normal."

"Apologize for what?"

"For makin' my life with my in-laws more miserable than it already was," she confessed in a bitter tone.

"This was all about you, huh? You didn't really want to see me."

She shook her head. "Of course I wanted to see you, too, Kerri. You're my own flesh and blood, even though sometimes I can't see how."

"Look, Mom," Britt cut our conversation short, "it's obvious they don't like Kerri, Kerri doesn't like them. I don't like them either, really. We paid our respects to Aunt Flora, we're out."

"Oh, Britt, can't you stay a few more hours, or even the night?"

Looked like this was a mother-son talk. I silently walked to the unlocked passenger's door, hoping Britt wouldn't give in to our mother's plea. *God, coming back here was a big mistake. Please don't let Britt change his mind about leaving.* I couldn't bear one more night at my parents' house with my dad's smoking and wheezing, my mom's fussing.

And now that Natalie had come in town and thoroughly embarrassed me, there was nothing left for us to do except bicker like the bitter enemies we'd become after years of trailing in my footsteps as the Dalee kid who wasn't quite as bright as the older two.

Even if Britt did decide to stay, I could ask Stephanie to transfer money to my checking account so I could get a hotel in the city or maybe even a flight back to Dallas and a cab home from the airport.

No, no, no. I had to stop relying on Stephanie to get me out of jams. I was twenty-four years old. A grown-up, and grown-ups knew how to stand on their own two feet without crawling back to people for help. Of course, Stephanie wouldn't make it feel like crawling. But, sooner or later, I knew Ricardo would.

The fight between Uncle Hugh and Lance made it to the light of day as the mob otherwise known as my family pushed through the front door and past the porch.

There were three distinct groups now: Hugh's side, Lance's side, and the spectators. The spectators grew as neighbors quickly joined the fiasco.

I grabbed my cell phone from my purse and called 9-1-1.

"Nine one one, what's your emergency?"

"Hi, there's a fight going on outside on Hall Street."

"In Crookshaw?"

"Yes, ma'am."

The dispatcher asked, "Is anyone hurt?"

"No. Not really, but if you all don't send someone soon, there might be."

"What's your name?"

I really hadn't thought through this far. Did I really want to go on record as the one family member who called the police when there were thirty others who didn't see reason to involve the law? Despite confidentiality laws, Crookshaw was a small town. My name wasn't safe with this woman.

"I…I don't want to give my name. Just hurry up and get here." I pressed 'END' before she could ask me any more questions.

Thankfully, Britt hopped into the car only moments later. We hightailed it to the highway, passing a patrol car on the side road.

Britt chewed on the side of his cheek for the first half-hour, listening to more 90's music. Then, out of nowhere, he asked, "So, what really happened with you and Uncle Billy?"

I felt like he'd just jabbed me in the stomach. "I don't want to talk about it."

Britt ran fingers through his hair a few times and took his eyes off the road for a second. "You know I'll believe you, right?"

No, I hadn't known. Never really crossed my mind that someone in my family might actually believe me before then.

"Really?"

"Totally. Uncle Billy should have been confined a long time ago. I can't think of a man who deserved to die in a construction accident more than him."

Just then, I realized why Britt would believe me. "Did he try something with you, too?"

"No. But he was creepy and all us kids knew it. He was always trying to show magazine pictures to us older boys. We wanted to see the naked ladies. I mean, what thirteen-year-old boy doesn't? But he had other magazines, too weird to talk about. Made us all feel ashamed, only I couldn't say anything to mom and dad because we'd *wanted* to look at the pictures of the ladies. I couldn't rat on Uncle Billy without ratting everyone else out, too, you know?"

I exhaled. All this time I thought there was something about me that had caused Aunt Flora's husband to suddenly become attracted to me. "He tried to kiss me with his mouth open," I said to my big brother for the first time.

Britt frowned and shook his head. "I swear I wish you had told me."

"I told Dad," I said, "which led to his silence with Aunt Flora until Uncle Billy died."

"Yeah," he relented. "I guess you did the right thing. And Dad kept the peace, I guess. But still, I wish you had told me. I would have done something else to Uncle Billy."

A sense of admiration swept through me. "Something like what?"

"I don't know. Maybe I would have pee'd in his drink and told him about it after he drank it," Britt laughed.

"That's gross!"

"He deserved it and than some. Maybe the God you've been praying to felt the same way," Britt smiled.

"I don't think God goes around killing people in construction accidents." At least I hadn't heard of such in the few scriptures I'd read.

"Whatever. The world is a safer place with Uncle Billy gone, that's for sure."

I couldn't argue with Britt there.

"But your family is still crazy," he teased.

"It's *your* family, too!" I insisted.

He raised an index finger. "Dude, I'm changing my name."

"I can get married," I laughed.

Britt signaled to get onto the main highway, transporting us back to our respective homes. He turned up the volume and an old Brittney Spears hit flowed through the speakers.

By that point, I figured someone in my family had probably already been arrested or at least ticketed thanks, to my call to the police. Uncle Hugh would soon be on his way to get stitches if someone from my family didn't come up with another remedy for the wound.

The food from the church might make it through one round, but certainly not a second. And they could all go back to life as normal in Crookshaw.

I used to leave this town and wonder when they would accept me. Not this time, though. Truth was: they might not ever accept me. And, for the first time, I was okay with that.

"Turn it up louder, Britt."

I don't know if God jams to Brittney Spears's music or not, but in my heart, I thanked Him for doing something in my heart, to the tune of *...Baby One More Time*.

Chapter 11

Stephanie didn't have to re-explain her church trip to Ricardo. Sunday morning at 7:30, he was still out like a light and barely even knew she'd left the apartment. "He snores amazingly loud," she admitted to me on our way into the church.

"Oh, please. You haven't heard snoring until you've heard my dad," I disagreed, letting the spring breeze whip hair off my forehead.

She grabbed my arm, stopping us both in the middle of a stream of people headed toward the sanctuary. "Hey? Look at me.

"What? Is there something in my nose?" I sniffed furiously.

"No," she said, smiling. "This is, like, the first time you've ever talked about your family without your eyebrows pinched together.

"All I said was my dad snores."

"Yeah," she nodded, "but you're not mad about it. This is huge. Seriously, you've delayed your Botox treatments by another five years."

Before church started, we made a pit stop so Stephanie could see my desk. "Your very own workspace!" she shrieked. She grabbed her iPhone from her white patent leather Kate Spade cross-body bag. She snapped a shot of my office, captioned it, and uploaded it to Facebook in record time. "You have arrived, Kerri!"

"Arrived to a *cubicle*?"

Her phone dinged before she could answer me. She glanced at the screen. "It's my mom. She says she's so proud of you and good luck."

Even though the good luck wishes hadn't come from my mom, I found it comforting to have someone over the age of forty think fondly of me.

"You should probably turn that phone off before we go inside," I warned her.

We made another stop in the restroom to check ourselves. Stephanie's slight curves caused her black sequin shell to catch the light in all the right places. She'd coupled the shirt with a pin-striped, fluffy skirt. I never would have thought to wear those two pieces together, but somehow they worked on Stephanie. Come to think of it, nothing she wore matched until she put it on. Then, I was like, "*Of course* that goes together! *Duh!*"

I, on the other hand, wore brown slacks with a brown button-down blouse. I had picked both garments from the same rack. Kind of like Garanimals.

Stephanie's long mystery-black hair and startling eye shadow skills caught the attention of a male usher, who escorted us clear up the front right section. Good grief! I was used to being treated special while in her company, but at church too?

"Hidden hotness," she whispered to me as we sidestepped between the first and second pew.

Just then, I noticed Stephanie smoothed her skirt against the back of her thighs before she sat. This must have been another one of those Junior Club etiquette tips that escaped me in Crookshaw.

Suddenly, I wondered what else everyone in the world knew except me. Granted, I hadn't worn many dresses in my twenty-four years, but I had never once run my hand along my backside before sitting in one. No, I was a plopper-downer.

Who am I kidding? I'm not normal. I don't have loving parents or a brilliant bilingual fiancé. If I don't know something as simple as how to sit down in a dress. I have no business working in my very own cubicle at this huge, swanky church. I'm nothing but a pretender.

Still, skirt-plopping pretender that I was, I had a job to do.

All at once, music played and the congregation stood.

"Good morning!" from a heavyset man with a microphone. "Praise the Lord!"

I recognized him from the previous Sunday. "Just watch the words on the screens."

The song-leader-man jumped right into a slew of songs. Stephanie seemed perfectly comfortable singing along with the crowd. I even saw her raise her hands when one of the musicians gave the directive.

"This is kind of like a concert," she echoed my initial observations. "Cool!"

After the singing, there was a brief baby christening ceremony. Four families brought their little ones to the altar and Pastor Scott dedicated them. He asked the church members to participate by verbally agreeing to support the family as they raised their children in the fear of the Lord.

Stephanie "oooohed" and "aaaawed" the whole time and even took a picture of one of the babies.

"What are you doing?" I asked her.

"Sending this to my mom and asking her if I was christened."

"I'm sure you were," I said. Most normal people have normal stuff done to them when they're little, I figured, which would explain why I'd never even witnessed a christening before that morning.

Stephanie's phone vibrated during the offering. She quickly nudged me and set the phone between us. There, on the screen, was a picture of Stephanie's parents on either side of baby Stephanie. Even then, her attire was spectacular.

"Cute."

She texted her mom, then put the phone away again just in time for Pastor Scott to take the podium. Quickly, I grabbed two pens and two spirals from my purse. Stephanie grabbed the set I offered her. We perched Bibles on our knees and assumed the position as Pastor Scott instructed us to flip to Revelation chapter 21, verses one through four.

Man, those Bible tabs came in handy. I made a note on my pad to thank Irene.

Stephanie leaned into me. "Why is he starting at the end?"

"I don't know. I guess they skip around." So much for reading the next chapter in First Corinthians.

Stephanie whispered again. "The pastor is very distinguished-looking and handsome, you know, in an old man way."

"Yeah," I agreed. "You should see his wife."

She winked at me. "I love them already."

As Pastor Scott preached, I could only hope Stephanie was "getting" it. All this talk about heaven and the New Jerusalem escaped me. Once again, his sermon caused more confusion than anything. I made a list of questions:

What happened to the Old Jerusalem?
What happened to the old heaven? If it was heaven, why destroy it?
How are we supposed to survive without a sea?

How can a whole city be a bride? Who is in the city?

Since when does God want a wife?

If they're in heaven, why are they crying so much that God has to wipe their tears away?

I peeked at Stephanie's notes. Thank goodness I didn't see any question marks on her page.

I had just about given up on anything being answered when Pastor Scott acknowledged at least one of my questions almost verbatim. "If you want to know the reason why the people of God, the very bride of Christ is crying as they enter into heaven, you must go back to the chapter twenty. Let's look at verse eleven."

He proceeded to read the text, adding points that were, somehow, clearer to me than what he had expounded upon earlier. Before the wonderful stuff happened in chapter 21, some bad stuff happened in chapter 20. People—apparently the majority of humanity—got separated from God, forever.

"They will never know His love again. Never, ever hope again. I submit to you, my brothers and sisters that we will first weep when our loved ones who did not accept Christ are removed from the New Jerusalem."

Stephanie's knee started bouncing.

"I realize that many if not most of us here today have accepted Christ as Savior. But we have friends, family members, co-workers, neighbors who have not. Some of them will be lost, forever. But they don't have to be. They can come to Jesus. He wants to take them as His bride, forever."

Soft music began to play as Pastor Scott closed his Bible and stepped front and center. "If you are already a believer, I encourage you to share Christ with those you love. If you're not a believer, but you want to know this Jesus, this Savior who died for your sins and will come again to receive you as His bride, come. He wants to love you forever. Come. "

Before I knew it, Stephanie had shot down our row and headed straight to the front of the sanctuary. She nearly collapsed at the steps leading to the podium, her body shaking with sobs. Several women surrounded her, rubbing her back and comforting her.

For some reason, my eyes became water faucets at the sight of my best friend losing it. Stephanie wasn't a crier. She was an over-the-top optimist. Something had to be devastatingly awful for her to cry.

After Pastor Scott prayed a prayer, Stephanie and the other people who had come to the altar walked back to some kind of special room. I didn't think I could go in the special room, so I simply sat down and fidgeted in my seat while I waited for her after dismissal.

I wiped my own tears from my eyes, thinking about what Pastor Scott had said. And the more I thought, the more I realized I shouldn't be crying anxious tears. I should be happy because now I wouldn't have to see Stephanie get separated from the rest of the Christians—assuming I was a Christian by just saying those words in the restroom.

I didn't get to talk to somebody in a designated room. I didn't cry like a baby when I met Jesus. Maybe I wasn't really a Christian at all. Maybe God would have to wipe Stephanie's eyes when *I* got banished from this New Jerusalem, which is apparently a lot better than the Old Jerusalem on the map now.

I bowed my head the way I saw many of my co-workers do before they ate. *God, I'm happy for Stephanie, I think, but what about me?*

"Kerri?"

Startled, I jumped in my seat.

"I'm sorry. I didn't mean to scare you," Irene apologized.

"Oh, it's okay. I was just…thinking. My best friend, Stephanie, is back there in, you know," I held up finger quotations, "the room."

"The room?"

"Yeah, with the people who went down the aisle."

"Wonderful! You see, God is already using you to bring others into the fold. I thank God for you. He works all things for the good of those who love Him."

I pursed my lips and pondered a churchy comeback. "Amen."

"So, did you get many notes?" she asked.

I shook my head. No need in waiting until five o'clock to give her the bad news. "No. Just a ton more questions. I'm sorry. I don't know all this stuff—"

She glinted with pleasure. "Great! You know, we used those questions you asked last week to create a frequently asked question section at the end of the post. They were wonderful. We got more hits on Pastor's sermon page last week than we've had in a long time.

"Seems you're not the only one with questions, Kerri. You're just the only one brave enough to ask them."

She stood there, probably waiting for another answer. I gave another pat reply. "God is good."

"Yes, He is."

Stephanie cried the whole way home.

"It's gonna be okay," I tried to console her.

"I know. That's what's so good about it." She had a goofy, drunk look about her that I didn't quite recognize.

"So why are you crying?" I asked her.

"Because He loves me. Don't you see?" She squinted and another set of tears rolled down her cheeks. "Everything that's happened—my parents christening me, my grandma taking me to church, us becoming best friends in college, you getting this job, me going to church with you and finding out I had already been given to God a long time ago on the morning I found out about Jesus? It's not a coincidence. It's like a twenty-four-year-long novel God's been writing all of my life. But I knew it. I knew there was something really big happening. I just didn't know what until today."

Wow.

I fixed my eyes on the road, wondering why God hadn't written a great fairy-tale love story for me.

Chapter 12

Ricardo met us at the door an immediately went into fix-it-man mode. "Steph, what's wrong?"

She grabbed his waist and squeezed him. He returned the hug, giving me a quizzical glance over her shoulder. I smiled and nodded to ease his mind a bit.

Ricardo pulled back and ducked down to look her in the eyes. "What's wrong?"

She shook her head. "Nothing's wrong. Everything's right. I met Jesus today and He saved me."

Ricardo's shoulders suddenly slumped. "Seriously?"

"Yes! And I can't wait for you to meet Him, Ricardo!" She threw both hands in the air and twirled through the kitchen to the living area, leaving Ricardo and I to stare at one another.

"Yes! Yes! Yes!" she sang aloud.

Ricardo and I trailed her, slowly. We both stopped in the kitchen, watching Stephanie dump herself onto the couch. This time, she didn't press her skirt onto her legs.

"What have you done to her?" Ricardo whispered, his dark complexion shadowed by a slight beard.

"I didn't do anything. It was…Jesus."

"There's no such freakin' thing as Jesus," he hissed.

Granted, I was not the authority on God, Jesus, or anything in the Bible, but something had happened to my best friend. And if she said it was Jesus, I believed her. "There *is* something bigger than all of us, you know?"

He pulled at two fistfuls of his own hair and yelled in Stephanie's direction, "No! There's nothing bigger than us. We're just people living our lives, alright? There is no God, no Jesus, no aliens, no Bigfoot, no tooth fairy, no Santa Clause, it's just *us*!"

Stephanie gingerly raised her head off the couch. I'm fully aware that no one has used the word "gingerly" in, like, a hundred years, but that's exactly the right word. She wasn't angry or sad, simply tender. She rested her hand on the arm of the chair, then her chin on her hand, making a bee-line from her eyes to Ricardo's.

"Do you really mean those words?"

"Uh, yeah," he chirped. "And if it wasn't for your jobless loser friend, here, brainwashing you, we wouldn't even be having this conversation."

Call me slow, but it took a moment for me to realize he'd just called me a loser. "Loser?"

"Yes, a loser." The words came hot and forceful as he tore his gaze from Stephanie to me. "You've been living off Stephanie's money and her brain for years. Figures the one time you actually find a job, you have to lie your way into it. I won't let you pull Stephanie into your fiction. I love her too much."

For a moment, I'd forgotten Stephanie was even in the room. Ricardo could just as well have been my father, spouting off a slew of thoughts that only confirmed the very thoughts I'd heard inside myself all my life. Everyone except Stephanie and, maybe, Irene had a list of my issues.

Stephanie stood across the bar from us and crossed her arms, huffing wildly, "Ricardo--"

"It's about time someone said it, okay?" he interrupted. "She's been riding your coattail long enough."

Then he turned to me. "I'm sorry if I hurt your feelings, Kerri, but it's time for us all to grow up and stop believing life's a bed of roses. Let's quit this church business and move on with real life," he concluded.

"First of all, Kerri is not a loser. She's the best friend I ever had. She's one of the few people on the planet who likes me for who I am, not because she sees money signs written all over my face," Stephanie yelled.

"Whatever! I'm your new best friend. We're about to be married."

"But," Stephanie chuckled, "we're getting *married* in a church."

"Yeah," he shrugged, "everyone gets married in a church but no one actually *believes* it. It's tradition."

"I do," she stated.

Ricardo threw his head back. "Oh, great, here we go. I've got a church lady for a wife. What's next? You gonna put on fifty pounds, start wearing long black skirts and run off to help orphans in Africa?"

"I might," she laughed. "I might do all of those things…except for the long black skirt…but don't you see the irony in all this? We're getting married at the church before God and witnesses, and you don't believe in the God we're standing before?"

"No, and it does not matter," he slowly enunciated.

Stephanie posed, "What if…what if I want our kids christened?"

"Uh, that's gonna be a no. We're not shoving religion down our kids' throats," he countered. Again, he faced me. "See what you've done? You're ruining everything."

"Leave her alone," Stephanie yelled.

I'd been standing there with my mouth open so long I forgot I had no business in the middle of their heart-to-heart conversation, let alone physically standing on Ricardo's side of the bar. "I'm out of here."

I nearly ran to my room, slamming the door behind me and throwing myself on my bed. This was supposed to be a harmless Christian job. Stephanie was supposed to help me take notes on Pastor Scott's sermon. Now, she was a *real* Christian and I was…a *bathroom* Christian. A pre-marital, home-wrecking *bathroom* Christian.

Ricardo and Stephanie argued into the afternoon. I drowned out their actual words with Pink's music blaring through my eardrums. Her music made me feel empowered. Like a roaring woman instead of a purring kitten.

But nothing could have prepared me for the awful, sinking feeling that rushed through me when I felt Ricardo's footsteps rush past my room and toward the front entry. He closed the main door behind him with such force I was certain the person beneath our apartment would have management call us the next day.

Stephanie sent me a text.

Wedding postponed. What Ricardo said about u and Jesus = not true. Want 2 b alone. Talk 2 u 2mrow. Nite.

Chapter 13

Monday morning, I managed to get a peek into Stephanie's bedroom before heading out to work. "You alright?"

"No. But I will be," she sighed. "I talked to my mom. She says if Ricardo can't respect my belief system or my friends, he's not the one for me."

I knew then that Stephanie would be okay. It must be nice to have a mother to talk to about your problems. "She's right."

"I know," Stephanie wailed, "I love Ricardo. But I know Jesus has been waiting a long, long time for me."

A smile blossomed on the inside of me for her. What a wild and crazy romance she had with Him already.

Thank goodness I arrived to work early. The monthly employee meeting started at eight o'clock sharp, clear on the other side of the church campus. Imagine my surprise to see my name on the program under the "New Employees" agenda item.

I found a seat next to Irene in what I now understood to be the youth sanctuary. The splash carpeting and flashy lighting system mimicked a 70's disco club if you asked me, but hey—kids today, you know?

"I'm sorry I forgot to tell you about this yesterday," Irene said. "We have the meeting on the first Monday of every month."

"No worries."

"Great. I'll be introducing you to the crew. Is there anything in particular you want everyone to know about you?"

Other than the fact I might be an imposter? "No, I can't think of anything worth sharing."

Irene winked at me.

I didn't like the looks of her wink.

A quick survey of the room revealed the magnitude of this church operation. Really, we could have been a small sampling of the church congregation; people from all corners of the city.

I could hardly pay attention to the program, seeing as the moment of introduction was coming up. Would I have to stand? Speak? Raise my right hand and pledge to something else I didn't understand?

Somehow, I felt better when a lady whom I recognized as the pastor's wife finally got up to walk us through my much-anticipated portion of the meeting. She had a sweetness about her, same as Irene. I wished I could call her sometime and tell her about my problems like Stephanie did with her mom.

For a moment, I got lost in the fantasy. What if Pastor and Mrs. Scott had been my parents? Then I could have had a normal life and grown up knowing about Jesus.

"Next, I'd like to allow Irene Trenton to introduce a young lady who has been especially helpful already with her writing gift."

Here we go. Irene stood and motioned for me to follow suit.

"I'd like to introduce Kerri Dale. She's new to our department and new to the faith, but already the Lord has used Kerri to bring more traffic to our website, and to bring her best friend to Christ."

The room roared with applause.

Irene continued, "Kerri, we want to welcome you to Wesley Street Bible Fellowship. We also welcome you to the body, the family of Christ. We're not perfect, but our Father is. And He is working to complete us all in Him."

Again, they clapped for me. In that moment, I wanted to let them take me in. I already knew Mary, Pike, Audra, and, of course, Irene. But the rest of these…people. Family? In Christ? Did we all have the same last name?

Surely, my grin was more a grimace. If only they knew.

Soon enough, Mrs. Scott was on to the next newcomer. I could breathe again.

Another lady wearing a Christmas hat drug a huge box onto the stage and introduced herself as Lulu. "I know it's the wrong time of year for this hat, but I feel like Santa Claus today," she bubbled with laughter.

"Grace and More Publishing has donated five hundred journals to our congregation, and Pastor Scott has asked me to distribute the journals by departments. You can use them as prizes during your ministry meetings, incentives for employees, or however you wish. They're just absolutely gorgeous."

Lulu held up one for all to see. Everyone gawked, including me. Every writer has a thing for pens and journals. I wished we'd done some kind of raffle because when it came to stuff like door prizes, I was pretty lucky.

The meeting lasted only an hour. Formalities. Once Pastor Scott prayed the closing prayer, most of my co-workers scattered off to their respective offices, presumably. Irene and I hung around for a while as she introduced me to even more employees.

Out of nowhere pops a guy whose voice carried a familiar ring. He was clean-cut, six feet, slightly husky, like maybe he was a linebacker in college but hadn't made the effort to lose the weight yet. No matter. He could be hidden hotness.

"Hi. It's nice to finally meet you, Kerri."

We shook hands. "Should I...know you?"

"I'm Jeremiah. The I-T guy. I helped set up your email account last week."

"Oh, yeah," I remembered, "thanks!"

"I'm just doing my job. Welcome to Wesley Street."

"Thank you. It's good to be here." *I think.*

He lingered long enough for me to figure out that he would have said more if Irene hadn't been standing there. My gosh, she really was a mother hen, in a good way.

Irene and I finally made it back to our side of Wesley Street and got back to work. A little before lunch, she rapped on my door. Well, I guess I should say she tapped on the metal frame of my cube.

I looked away from the children's ministry newsletter I'd been proofing. "Yes?"

"Got something for you." She produced one of the coveted journals from behind her back. "Tada!"

"Oh wow! Thanks!"

"I saw the look in your eyes when Lulu held up the sample."

"Was I that obvious?"

Irene laughed. "Uh, yeah."

She transferred ownership of the journal from her hands to mine. I ran my fingers along the leather spine with gold embossing at the top and bottom.

This thing could have easily been mistaken for a small Bible, were it not for the magnetic flap across the front to keep it closed. "Thank you."

"You're welcome, Kerri. I hope it will add to your prayer life."

A sarcastic laugh escaped my throat.

She asked, "What was that for?"

"Irene, I don't have a prayer life. I don't even know if I have a Christian life." I was on a roll. "My best friend just bawled at the altar yesterday. She totally changed, I mean, really, she's probably going to call off her wedding because she fell in love with Jesus. That didn't happen to me so…I mean…I want to know Him like she does, but I don't."

Irene leaned against the metal. Lowered her hands, laced her fingers. "Maybe Jesus had to make a drastic change in her yesterday because there was no time to lose."

"But I wish He would do that for *me*. I want Him to speak to *my* heart and tell *me* He loves me the way He did Stephanie." I could hardly breathe as tears blurred my vision. "I want Jesus. I *want* Him."

Irene approached me and put a hand on my shoulder. "And He wants you, too, Kerri."

"But how do I find Him? How do I *get* Him?"

"Oh, trust me. He's already drawing you to Him. Just talk to Him." She pointed at the journal. "Write to Him. He'll respond in your heart." She winked at me for the second time. "I'll be praying for you."

With that, she left my workspace. Part of me had wanted her to hug me and tell me everything would be okay, that I was loved and already a Christian. But I'd watched Irene long enough to know she wasn't interested in me getting closer to her. She wanted me to get close to Him.

So, I followed her advice. I found the nearest private spot, which wasn't my office. Not with so many people walking by, saying how proud they were that I'd led my friend to Christ. They acted as though I'd done something most Christians didn't do.

Nonetheless, I snuck away from my desk and down the hall in search of a private spot. The ladies' room. It seemed only right for me to re-enter the very same stall to try and get this thing right.

I made sure the top was dry, then rested on the seat.

I opened that journal and told Jesus exactly what I needed Him to know.

Dear Jesus,

It's me. Kerri Dalee (rhymes with Bailey). We met here, in this restroom a little while back. Then, I just wanted a job. But now, I want you. I've done a lot of stuff wrong and my family didn't even acknowledge you, so I need like super-quadruple forgiveness. Please come into my heart, be my God like you did with Stephanie and all those people in the Bible. Show me all that stuff in the Bible, too, because it's Greek to me. (I think maybe some parts of the Bible were written in Greek, so I guess it's okay.)

Anyway, I'm so sorry about this whole bathroom thing. Let's start over.

-Kerri

And that's how I met Him in the ladies' room. Again.

~

If you liked *I Met Him in the Ladies' Room*, meet
Mama B!

An Excerpt from Mama B:
A Time to Speak
A Novella by Michelle Stimpson

Through the sheer part of my curtains, I could
see two figures sitting on my porch bench. A woman
and a little boy. I paused for a second, had to think of
who they might be.

Then I caught onto her voice as she fussed at
the child. "Cameron, this is the last time I'm going to
tell you to tie your shoes correctly. You don't want
Mama B to think you eight years old and can't even
tie your shoes right, do you?"

"No ma'am."

Cameron. Nikki. I should have known
something was going on with those two as much as
the Lord had been bringing them up in my Spirit. My
mind didn't even have time to ask the questions
before I found myself outside again, on that porch
hugging them.

"Mama B," she nearly cried as she pulled me
into her embrace, "I'm so glad to see you."

"Me, too, Nikki-Nik!" Inside, my heart was
bubbling over with joy. Nikki, my oldest grandbaby,
come to Peasner to see me.

"And look at you, Cameron! Oh, you look so
much like your grandfather, it's a shame!"

He didn't say anything, just stood there with a
little shy smile on his face.

My granddaughter looked good. Like she'd been taking care of herself. Light brown skin, just like her Daddy, button nose like her mother. Got the kind of hair can straighten out with just a blow dryer. Toes done, nails done. Been taking care of herself.

Cameron looked well, too, though he was still holding on to quite a bit of baby fat. No matter, I'd rather have him too plump than too skinny any day. *Thank You, Lord, for keeping them in Your care.*

After all our greeting, I took a step back from them. "Does your father know you're here?"

She smacked her lips, whispered so Cameron wouldn't hear us. "Mama B, you know my daddy don't talk to me."

Son said the same thing about her. I could tell Nikki didn't really want to talk about her father. "How's your mother?"

Her face smoothed back out again. "She's fine. You know my Momma—off seeing the world. She went on a cruise with some of her friends to celebrate their fiftieth birthdays."

"She know you're here?"

"Yes, ma'am."

I glanced behind Nikki and saw four bulging suitcases parked on my wooden porch planks.

"Sweetie, you planning on staying in Peasner for a spell?"

She looked up at me with her slanted, brown eyes—same as my husband's and her father's. Real fast, she darted those eyes away from me. "Mama B, I'm in a really bad situation right now. We need to stay with you...for just a little while."

Freeze. I done heard *that* one plenty of times before. Peoples evicted for not paying rent, wives leavin' their cheatin' husbands, teenagers not getting along with their parents. Every time, I listen. Wait for the Holy Spirit to tell me what to do because I don't want to call myself trying to help somebody but end up hindering what God really wants to do in their life.

Some folk need a few good homeless, hungry, sleepless nights to make the voice of God real clear. Other folk need a soft bed and a warm meal before they can hear Him. He knows, and He has to let me know, too.

Now, I have to be honest and say the first thing came to my mind wasn't nothin' from the Lord. I was thinking about me and all the stuff I didn't want to have to put up with like an eight-year-old running around my house and a twenty-something year-old doing whatever it is they do. Share my TV. Plus I gotta cook for three now. I know Nikki old enough to cook for herself, but I might as well go ahead and cook for everybody long as I'm in the kitchen already.

What else? Gotta wait for some more hot water before I take my shower. Water bill, power bill, gas bill higher.

All this is coming from me, now, and I'm waiting on the Holy Spirit to agree with my thoughts, but He didn't. And since the Lord didn't co-sign on my veto, I had no choice except to put myself aside; wait until He say something different. Wasn't for Him and Albert's life insurance, I wouldn't have a place to rest my head, either. *Thank You, Lord, for a home that I can share.*

Unfreeze.

"You and Cameron get those suitcases and come on in here. I've got something for us to eat already."

"Thank you, Mama B."

I should have known the first words out of Cameron's mouth would be pertaining to food. "What'd you cook?"

"Turkey stew."

He had the nerve to draw up his face. "Turkey stew?"

"Yes, sir, with lots of vegetables. Chocolate cake for dessert."

A big smile spread across his chubby little face; cheeks just begging for a kiss and a pinch. "I like chocolate cake."

I can tell. "Only after you finish your stew."

At my word, they followed me to Debra Kay and Cassandra's old bedroom. Since I mentioned dessert, apparently Cameron became my best friend. "Mama B," he said, breathing hard as he rolled suitcases down the hallway, "does the cake have frosting?"

"Sure does. Chocolate on chocolate." Wouldn't be no extra food to give away so long as he was around.

After they set down their suitcases, we all washed up and met at the kitchen table to eat. I blessed the food and asked the Lord to make Nikki's time with me profitable for His sake. We all said amen and started eating.

I love my grands, but letting people move in with you always bring some kinda problem. Might be a big problem, might be a little problem. But it's always a problem, that's for sure.

Other Books by the Michelle Stimpson

Fiction

Boaz Brown

Divas of Damascus Road

Falling into Grace

Last Temptation (Starring "Peaches" from *Boaz Brown*)

Mama B – A Time to Speak

Someone to Watch Over Me

The Good Stuff

Trouble In My Way (Young Adult)

Non-Fiction

Did I Marry the Wrong Guy? And other silent ponderings of a fairly normal Christian wife

Visit Michelle online:

www.MichelleStimpson.com

About the Author

In addition to her work in the field of education, Michelle ministers through writing and public speaking. Her works include the highly acclaimed *Boaz Brown*, *Divas of Damascus Road* (National Bestseller), and *Falling Into Grace,* which has been optioned for a movie of the week. She has published several short stories for high school students through her educational publishing company.

Michelle serves in women's ministry at her home church, Oak Cliff Bible Fellowship. She also ministers to women and writers through her blog. She regularly speaks at special events and writing workshops sponsored churches, schools, book clubs, and educational organizations.

The Stimpsons are proud parents of two young adults and one crazy dog.

Made in the USA
Lexington, KY
31 March 2018